"How Did I Get Mixed Up In This Stupid Scheme?"

He raised his eyes to the ceiling. "Why me?"

"I thought—I thought—" she sniffed, "you had some compassion."

"Compassion?" He laughed. "Me?" And then his eyes turned serious again. "Just because I won't be the father of your child."

"I'm not asking you to." She lifted her chin and that curious dimple appeared. "All I'm asking is for you to be my husband, for awhile."

"Why?"

"For Eric's sake," she whispered.

CAROLYN THORNTON
combines a southern heritage with her love for far away places she encountered while writing travel articles. She states that "the question *what if* led me to write the kind of novel I enjoy reading."

Dear Reader:

Silhouette has always tried to give you exactly what you want. When you asked for increased realism, deeper characterization and greater length, we brought you Silhouette Special Editions. When you asked for increased sensuality, we brought you Silhouette Desire. Now you ask for books with the length and depth of Special Editions, the sensuality of Desire, but with something else besides, something that no one else offers. Now we bring you SILHOUETTE INTIMATE MOMENTS, true romance novels, longer than the usual, with all the depth that length requires. More sensuous than the usual, with characters whose maturity matches that sensuality. Books with the ingredient no one else has tapped: excitement.

There is an electricity between two people in love that makes everything they do magic, larger than life—and this is what we bring you in SILHOUETTE INTIMATE MOMENTS. Look for them wherever you buy books.

These books are for the woman who wants more than she has ever had before. These books are for you. As always, we look forward to your comments and suggestions. You can write to me at the address below:

Karen Solem
Editor-in-Chief
Silhouette Books
P.O. Box 769
New York, N.Y. 10019

CAROLYN THORNTON
For Eric's Sake

Silhouette *Romance*

Published by Silhouette Books New York

America's Publisher of Contemporary Romance

Other Silhouette Books by Carolyn Thornton

The Heart Never Forgets
Love Is Surrender
Pride's Reckoning
Looking Glass Love

SILHOUETTE BOOKS, a Simon & Schuster Division of
GULF & WESTERN CORPORATION
1230 Avenue of the Americas, New York, N.Y. 10020

ISBN: 0-671-57229-6

First Silhouette Books printing, June, 1983

10 9 8 7 6 5 4 3 2 1

Map by Ray Lundgren

For Eric's Sake

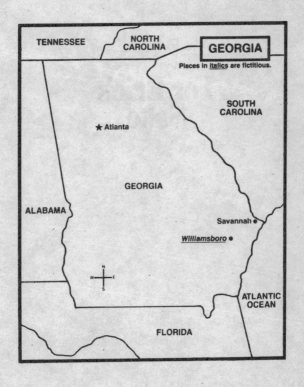

TENNESSEE

NORTH CAROLINA

GEORGIA

Places in _italics_ are fictitious.

SOUTH CAROLINA

★ Atlanta

GEORGIA

ALABAMA

Savannah ●

Williamsboro ●

N
W   E
S

ATLANTIC OCEAN

FLORIDA

Chapter One

Brandy Logan looked down at the dark, masculine head lying on her breast and wondered how she was going to explain *her* presence in *his* bed.

He stirred, and snuggling closer, threw an arm across her bare midriff. Beneath his hand she felt a funny sensation deep within her body. Although not unpleasant, it was unfamiliar and frightening.

Oh God, she prayed, trying to ignore the reaction of her body to his caressive touch, *help me to be convincing.*

For Eric's sake.

Slowly he awakened, his thumb moving circularly over her hip, across to her navel, then lower. Breathlessly curious, she waited for his next move, wondering what all the subtleties of lovemaking involved. She had to keep a strict control on herself. His hands alone could cause her to forget her purpose. Reason reminded her he had probably made love to many women. For him, she was just another body.

She wriggled away from him, dragging the sheets up around her neck.

He came fully awake and smiled up at her. "Morning, beautiful."

Brandy smiled a bit uncertainly, wondering how much of last night he remembered. At least he wasn't surprised to find her in his bed, but then, he probably *never* slept alone. She guessed he wouldn't be smiling at her right now if he recalled the circumstances which led *them* to *this* bed.

Her heart pounded so rapidly she thought he would surely see the action through the thin barrier of the sheet. "Good morning," she whispered and turned away, embarrassed by the look in his green eyes.

He laughed, and reached up to touch her cheek with the back of his hand. "I didn't think women blushed anymore," he said.

"Why not?" she asked. *Anything to keep him talking,* she thought. If she didn't, he might take up where he left off last night.

"Women's lib," he answered, cocking his head, admiring her deep set brown eyes, full lips and soft dark brown hair framing her sensuous face. "You women are so busy trying to even the numbers, hopping in and out of bed with whoever is conveniently near, that there's very little mystery left, and certainly nothing to blush about."

Her color deepened as he spoke. She was guilty, but

not in the way he thought. "I don't sleep around," she asserted.

"You spent the night with me." His eyes sparkled with amusement.

She wanted to slap the grin off his face, but remembered he would soon be angry enough. She lamely answered, "That was different."

"Hmmm. That's what they all say." His hands found her body again beneath the covers. Brandy wished she were at least wearing the slight protection of a nightgown. She had never slept in the nude, or even with a man before, but she couldn't tell him that. It was all part of her scheme.

"Please," she whispered, half of her loving the way his hand smoothed around the curves of her body where no man had touched her before.

"Please what?" he asked huskily, and pulled her up against the length of his hard warm body, taking her lips with his own.

Brandy wanted to put her arms around his neck and pull him down to her as his lips left hers to travel across her cheek and nibble at her ear. But she had to remember all of his moves were calculated for just that kind of reaction. He knew how to make women respond to him. His lovemaking was deliberate, calculated to satisfy his masculine image. Besides, she'd already gotten him where she wanted him. Now she had to convince him of the importance of her situation and why she had to stay there.

"Please what?" he prompted, his breath warm in her ear. "Please make love to you?"

Even his husky voice could set her body on fire with yearning. It would be so easy to give in to him, just for the moment; she had no doubt he would make every second pleasurable. But it would be selfish of her to invite him to continue, especially when there was Eric to consider.

"Please don't," she whispered, and wondered, when he didn't immediately stop his caressing and kissing, if he had heard her at all. She almost wished he hadn't.

Her body was hard with arousal, just as she could feel his own on top of her. His light touches made her wriggle with delight. It was as if he were strumming her like a fine musical instrument. She lifted her arms from beneath the covers to pull him even closer to her, wanting more than he was giving, but not understanding what she was asking.

As the flat of her palms came in contact with his smooth bare back rippling with muscles, he raised his head. His eyes, glazed with passion, stared into her own.

"What the hell—" he muttered, levering himself away from her and seizing her left hand to stare at the plain wide band he had felt when she touched his back.

Brandy blushed at the thought of how intimate he had become, and of how little she had done to stop him.

"Is that what I think it is?" His tone said it was a crime to wear a wedding ring, especially in his presence.

Brandy forced it up and down over her knuckle. "I am having a little trouble getting used to it. It's too tight."

He moved away from her as if he'd just discovered she had measles and was in the quarantine stage. "Look," he growled, "I may not think too much of marriage personally, but one thing I don't do is fool around with another man's wife."

Her heart pounded almost audibly. He did not remember all the details of the previous night. And he *did* have some set of standards. "It's okay. You don't have to worry about a jealous husband," she assured him.

"Now don't tell me he's out of town and will never find out. I wouldn't care if he's on the other side of the globe right now. I don't seduce married women. It's a principle with me."

Brandy wanted to smile. From what she'd heard about him, it seemed incongruous to hear Shaw Janus talk about principles where women were concerned. But the fact that she had glimpsed compassion in him had initially given her the courage to involve him in her problem—and maybe there *was* more to the man than his image implied. She was trusting enough to give him the benefit of the doubt. "That's very commendable of you," she said. If he noted the sarcasm in her voice, he didn't comment on it.

Instead he threw the covers back and pulled on his pants which lay discarded in a heap where he had stepped out of them the night before. "I must say though," he looked around the bedroom for the first time, "you have an exotic taste for decorating."

"What?" She was mesmerized by the sight of his athletic build, surprisingly unembarrassed by his nakedness: it was the way he moved with a self-assurance as if he were fully clothed. There was no reason for him to be shy. Countless women had no doubt watched him dress and undress, and many had probably even helped him.

"The mirrors. Erotic," he said.

"Oh," she said, realizing he didn't remember where they were. "This isn't my apartment."

He looked back at her huddled form beneath the covers of the bed. "No, I guess it wouldn't be. Not if hubby were expected home. But it sure isn't my place. Where are we?" He rubbed his head, and she wondered if he had a headache after all she had helped him drink the previous night.

"We're in a hotel," she explained, wondering how best to break the news to him of how and why they were there.

"Logical," he shook his head, his tousled, nut-brown hair making him look like a boy, "but not my style."

She didn't think it was. From the rumors she'd heard, he slept around. Women probably even came to *him* asking for a night in his bed. He should have nothing to hide, no reason to be discreet. "It's the bridal suite."

He turned and glowered at her in amazement. Then he fell back onto the bed and howled with laughter. "This is hilarious," he finally calmed down enough to say. "No woman's ever gotten me as far as the bridal suite before—and a married woman at that," he chuckled as he bent to pick up his shirt, stuffing the tails into his pants.

"I bet no woman's ever gotten you to the altar before last night either," she held her breath. It had been the one thing she hadn't been able to find out, whether or not he had ever been married.

"You're right about that," he grinned rakishly. As he looped his tie around his neck, he casually turned back to her, then suddenly, all amusement drained from his face, he asked cautiously, "What do you mean, 'before last night'?"

"Don't you remember?" she taunted, wanting to see him squirm for all his arrogance. The tables would be turned soon enough. She knew he was not the type of man to let a woman dominate him for long.

"Remember what?" he demanded.

"You asked me to marry you." She forced herself not to look away from him.

He was the one to break eye contact, while running a hand through his thick, curling hair. "I remember joking about marriage—vaguely. But look here," he glared at Brandy, "you can't take that seriously. I talk love to all the girls I go out with. And besides," he passed his hand through his hair again, "I can't for the life of me remember your name."

"How does Brandy Janus sound?" she asked, and concentrated deliberately on the ring on her left hand.

"Ridiculous," he spat, knotting his tie.

"I think so, too." She leaned back against the headboard of the bed, tucking the sheets around her. "I guess I'll keep my maiden name for professional reasons. You won't mind, will you, Shaw?"

"Why should I mind?" He jerked his tie tight. "What is this about your maiden name? What in hell are you babbling about?"

"You," she breathed, afraid to look directly at him, "and me. We were married last night."

He turned and stared at her for a long moment. Then he dismissed her with a smile, checking his wristwatch to see if it had stopped ticking. "I have to admit if I were going to take a wife, I'd choose someone as beautiful as you. But beauty wouldn't be the only thing

I'd want. And I'm not in the market for a wife at the moment," he stated, trying to close the subject.

Brandy wondered when he would want a wife. Why was he afraid of marriage? What did he need that he had not been able to find in a woman? "I did get that idea," she answered, "but *I* was in the market for a husband, and as strange as it may sound, you were the best I could come up with on short notice."

He laughed. "You have some cheek, I'll hand you that, but no woman has ever gotten the better of me."

"I'm not trying to win some sort of power play with you," she admitted. "I simply want to be married to you."

"A lot of women would," he said. "But just because you're a fan doesn't mean I'm going to be so grateful that I'll marry you."

"I'm not one of your fans." She shook her head. "I'm your wife."

"Well, it won't work."

Last night she had played the sly seductress. This morning she was dealing with hard facts. "I'm telling you, you already married me."

"It can't be legal," he claimed. "Nobody gets married overnight, except in movies. There are such things as blood tests, licenses, crossing state lines for a Justice of the Peace at the very least. I don't remember doing any of that!"

Brandy smoothed the sheets down around her, wondering if it would hurt to play the role of wronged virgin. A swift glance in his direction said it would. "I don't think you remember much of anything that happened last night. You do drink a lot, don't you?"

He remembered wanting her, wanting her so badly that he would have done almost anything to get her—

anything but marry her. "I was trying to keep up with you," he replied.

Brandy blushed. She had ordered drink after drink, but had dumped them out every chance she got. "Our marriage license is in my purse if you'd like to look at it," she offered.

"That I would." He looked around the room and spied her purse on the dresser near the bundle of her own discarded clothes. He crossed the room and picked it up.

As the reality of the situation washed over him, his face contorted with rage. "This is ridiculous. How did you manage all the details? There's a waiting period for the license."

"I got that last week."

His brows shot up. "But I only met you this week."

She nodded. "You were always too busy with other women last week to notice me."

He found that hard to believe. She was the kind of woman that stood out in a stadium of people, and he could understand how easily he had been attracted to her. Even now, looking at her suggestive form beneath the blankets of the bed, he wanted nothing more than to slip between the sheets again and—

But this was ridiculous. He couldn't be married to her! he thought. Glaring at her, he thrust his hands into his pockets. His fingers came in contact with a slip of paper he didn't remember putting there. He pulled it out, read it and waved it in the air. "This is from the blood test! How did you manage that?"

"I have a friend who works in a clinic. Don't you feel a little tenderness in your arm?" She rubbed her own. "I do."

His eyes grew wider and his irritation increased. He

had thought he was waking up with a dream girl, but it was all turning into a cruel nightmare.

"And the Justice of the Peace. Where did you find one on such short notice?" he demanded.

"It wasn't a Justice of the Peace," she sighed. "It was a minister."

"Geez," he exhaled, running a hand through his hair, and walking over to the window.

Brandy wondered if, while his back was turned, she should take that moment to slip out of bed and try to dress, but decided against it as every few minutes he sent her little shocked glances.

She heaved a sigh. She had pulled it off, managed to have him marry her, legally, against all the odds. Reverend Rourke had told her it would never work. He had advised against it, but had finally relented in the face of her determination. He had known how important it was for her to keep Eric, but he had also warned her how difficult it would be to get an annulment if the marriage turned out to be anything but in name only. Right now, she didn't want to speculate on whether or not she could stay married to Shaw Janus—she just hoped it would be long enough to keep Eric with her.

"Woman," he said, and she could tell he was talking through his teeth even though his back was to her, "I don't know how you managed such a stunt, but I'll find some way to undo it. Get the marriage annulled, or—"

"You can't do that," Brandy said softly, "not after it's been consummated." She didn't look up to see his reaction. She couldn't. If she did, he might get a hint of the truth: that he had been too drunk the night before to do anything but topple into bed and fall asleep; she was counting on that to have the marriage annulled.

But she would have to hold out until she was with

Eric for good. Now, Shaw Janus had to believe he had completely seduced her. She had to keep him married to her, for awhile at least.

"Then I'll divorce you if that's what it takes." His eyes flashed as he focused on her. "I don't want and I don't need a wife."

"How do you know," she asked, her eyes all innocence, "if you've never had one?"

"I don't need a wife," he repeated.

"But *I* need a husband." She lifted her eyes to him, tears glistening.

"Terrific!" He threw up his hands. "Some guy's gotten you pregnant and I get all the blame and the responsibility. Well, I don't like your games, little lady, and I won't be threatened or blackmailed."

"It's not like that at all," she whimpered.

"Don't sit there crying!" he shouted. "I can't stand crying. It won't score any points with me."

"I'm not doing it on purpose." She glared at him, holding her sobs within, but unable to control the tears slipping down her face. "Believe me, I wouldn't have involved you if there had been any other way."

"How did I get mixed up in this stupid scheme?" He raised his eyes to the ceiling. "Why me?"

"I thought . . . I thought . . ." she whispered, "you had some compassion."

"Compassion?" he repeated the word and laughed. "Me?" Then his eyes turned serious again. "I don't get women pregnant, and you can call that compassion if you like, but I will not be the father of your child."

"I'm not asking you to." She lifted her chin and a curious dimple appeared. "All I'm asking is for you to be my husband for awhile."

"Why?"

"For Eric's sake," she whispered.

"Who is Eric?" he thundered. "Is he the man who got you in trouble? Hasn't anyone taught him about living up to his own responsibilities?"

"Eric is a helpless little boy."

"He can't be all that helpless if he can make you pregnant."

"I'm not pregnant!" She tugged the sheets tighter around her.

"Then why do you need to get married?" Shaw thundered again.

"I told you, for Eric's sake."

He heaved a sigh, glared up at the ceiling, and said, "Suppose we start at the beginning?"

"Fine."

"Who's Eric?"

"I told you. He's a little boy."

"Whose little boy? Yours?" She didn't look old enough to have children, but it was possible that she could have a child. Several for that matter. But still, Shaw thought, she couldn't be more than twenty-one.

"He's my sister's little boy."

"All right." He sat down on the bed very calmly. "Now we're getting somewhere. Why did you feel you had to marry someone if Eric is your sister's boy?"

"Because she and Dick were killed in an accident a month ago and there's no one else to take care of him the way he should be cared for," Brandy explained.

"Who's Dick?"

"My sister's husband."

"What about your parents?" He frowned, knowing he was letting himself get involved.

"They're gone, too . . . when I was ten."

He didn't want to pry further, but asked, "No other relatives?"

"Well, yes, that's the point."

His brows peaked.

"My aunt and uncle, Louis and May Logan, want to take Eric."

"Good," he said, slapping his hands on his thighs. "The problem's solved then."

She shook her head. "You don't understand." Tears threatened behind her eyes again, and she reached out and touched his back. "Please."

She had said please to him already once this morning. He could still recall the warm seductive look of her, feel her silky smooth skin. "Please what?" he had asked.

"Please help me."

He wanted to bash his fists against a wall. He wanted to shout and kick and scream. He wanted to do anything but sit here and listen to her. A crazy feeling skittered up his spine. If he weren't careful, this girl would have him wrapped up like a Christmas package. There was something about the way she looked at him, not pleading, but proud, yet helpless and alone. "How can I help you?" he grated.

"By staying married to me long enough for the courts to turn Eric over to my care, long enough for Louis and May to stop fighting over Eric as if he were a chicken wishbone and long enough for them to leave the country and forget him. Louis is planning to move to Australia," she explained.

"I still don't see what's wrong with them taking him."

"He'd hate it." She raked her left hand—the hand

wearing his ring—through her sultry hair, reminding him that he *was* married to her, at least for the moment. It made him feel strange to know that he possessed this beautiful woman. No other man could lay claim to her while she wore his ring.

"Eric would hate living with them. They already have a brood of kids who don't get as much attention and love as they should. Louis and May are too busy flitting around the world to worry about their children having the security of going to the same school for even one whole year. Little Ginger went to four different schools during the first grade. Four! Can you imagine the insecurity of that? I hated school myself, but add being uprooted and having to make new friends each year—it's terrible! I don't want that to happen to Eric."

"How old is he?"

"Eric? He's six."

Shaw scratched his head while looking at her, reproaching himself for weakening. She had called it *compassion*, but he thought it was actually *stupidity*. He didn't want to get involved. "Why won't they just let you have him?" he asked.

"Because I was single." *Was*, he noted. "And particularly because of my career, they didn't think I'd be a good influence."

"What are you, a topless waitress or something?" He grinned. He could not remember how she looked naked, but he grew hot with the memory of the feel of her.

"No, a model. Or trying to be, at least," she replied.

That answer made him curiously angry, but he didn't know why.

"And they think I'm too young," Brandy added.

"How old are you?" he asked.

"Eighteen."

"Eighteen!" Shaw shouted disbelievingly. And he'd taken her to bed. Correction, he thought, he'd married her! Married her! It was almost like robbing the cradle. "Do you have any idea how old I am?"

"No. Should I?" she answered innocently.

"Yes! I'm thirty. And here I am married to an eighteen-year-old!" He stalked away from her to the window, hoping the real world was still outside the room.

"Does that mean, then, that you've accepted the fact that we are married?" she asked him hesitantly.

"I've accepted the *fact*, but not the responsibility," Shaw countered.

"Which means?"

"I don't know what it means. I've never found myself in this kind of situation before. I've avoided any implication of marriage. How in the world you managed all of this I'm still not certain," he said, shaking his head.

Someday she might explain all the details of how she had arranged to get the blood tests after hours at the clinic, picked up the wedding ring and the license a week ago and spent days pleading with Reverend Rourke to marry her because of the urgency of the situation. Someday she might be able to tell Shaw. But this was not the time.

"I won't get in your way. I won't try to make changes. I promise it will only be temporary," she assured him.

"I hope you don't expect me to be faithful to you?" What in the world was he saying? he asked himself. Was he actually considering this farce of a marriage with her?

She looked down, pleating the sheets between her fingers. "I realize I've interrupted your life, but it won't be for long. I promise. But you will be—"

She paused and he prompted. "What?"

"Discreet with your affairs. For appearances sake, for the courts?" she pleaded.

His eyes widened. No one had ever suggested he be *discreet,* and he couldn't believe his ears. It was ridiculous. It went against the grain of his principles. No woman had ever gotten the better of him and he had to hand it to her for not only attempting such a feat, but also for carrying it so far. Who was she to tell him what to do?

"Please?"

It was her eyes, great velvet pools of brown, that had snared him. Had she realized when she had planned all of this how susceptible he would be to them? Compassion, she had called it, but it was his own downright weakness.

Would it hurt to play her husband for awhile? he wondered. At least he knew, they *both* knew, it would be temporary, and he wouldn't mind a brief romance with her, although for the life of him he couldn't remember making love to her the previous night.

"What about my reputation?" he asked her. "A wife doesn't fit into my world—not even briefly."

"From what I've heard, your reputation could use a little stability." For the last week she had talked to everyone she could find who knew him, had spent evenings in all the nightspots he was known to frequent and had eaten dinner each night in his restaurant, The Pub. She had read back issues of the newspapers about his newest restaurant opening, and had even found a biography about him on file in the library, filled with gossip about his string of girlfriends. She thought she knew as much about him as anyone could, but that much had taught her no one knew him very well at all.

Shaw Janus' public life was a series of images projected to enhance the charisma of his personality: an up-to-date, '80's style man, who was conversant with radical life styles and live-together arrangements. His knowledge of both sides of an issue made it difficult to determine his personal viewpoints, but he always had an opinion, and was frequently asked for it by newspaper columnists. Still, she had discreetly watched him in action enough to detect a sense of fairness about him. And it was that sense of fairness that had convinced her he would take up her cause.

"Look, you don't know the first thing about me," he said.

She didn't answer. What he said was true enough. All she knew were generalities.

"I'm right in the middle of opening this new restaurant. For the first time in my life I'm getting where I want to go, but I'm not quite there yet, and a wife won't help the situation at all. I can't expect you to understand that. In fact, I don't think I even owe you an explanation if it comes to that, but just take my word for it. I don't want, and I don't need a wife," he repeated.

"Not even for a little while?"

"No," he snapped, and pulled on his socks and shoes. "I'm late for work already and I can see this conversation is going to take more than five minutes to iron out."

"Do you want me to stay here? Or shall I go home?"

"For God's sake go home. I don't want to pay for another night in the bridal suite. The first night was expensive enough."

Brandy suppressed a grin. He wasn't referring to the monetary expense of the room since they hadn't paid for it last night. And she knew he could well afford it. "Do you want to give me the key?" She held out her hand.

"The key? To what?" He jerked around to look at her.

"To your home, of course. I'll wait for you there."

"Look, I've been trying to tell you—oh, forget it." He dug around in his pocket and tossed it to her. "But don't get any ideas about moving in. Just be there when I get in this evening and we'll talk this thing through sensibly, like two adults, even though only one of us has reached that stage."

"Thanks." She smiled, her mind already racing ahead to decide how best she could win him over to her way of thinking.

"The address is—" he began.

"Oh, I know, thanks."

His eyes widened. What else did she know about him? he wondered. And who was she? He sat staring at her, his body growing hot at the thought of her body so warmly within his reach. Forget it, he told himself, shaking his head. That was probably how he got himself into this situation in the first place. No woman was going to seduce him—at least not a second time.

"What time will you be home?" she asked.

"Around six if things go well. I'll let you know if not." What *was* he doing, he wondered, giving her his schedule. Next thing he knew she'd have him neatly boxed into a timetable. He stood up, determined to get away from her. She had a strange effect on his rationality. "I'll pay the bill on my way down, if I have enough cash on me," he muttered. No telling how much he had spent on her during the previous evening.

"Shaw." She stopped him as he went to the door.

He turned back to her. "What?"

"Thanks."

"Don't thank me. I haven't done anything, and I don't intend to. So don't get any ideas about homemaking."

"Thanks for at least listening."

"I'll see you tonight." He turned on his heel and left her lying naked in the bed in which they had spent the night—alone in the bridal suite on the first morning of their marriage.

Chapter Two

Brandy stared at the door long after Shaw had shut it behind him. She wanted to be certain he was gone before she left the protective cocoon of bed covers. In some ways she was just as shocked as he that she had carried through her wild scheme. But she had been forced to—for Eric's sake.

The plain gold band looked out of place on her left hand. It would probably tarnish or turn her finger green before the week was out, but it had been the only one she could afford at the time. What did it matter how it looked as long as it was there—an acknowledgment of her marriage for the world to see?

Marriage. Brandy's sight blurred. All her childhood romantic illusions about courtship, a white dress and a loving husband had been shattered. She had not had time for any of that, and now she might not ever have a chance for love. She would never again be able to imagine herself as a blushing bride, because once she acquired custody of Eric, she would be labeled "divorced" forever.

A tear dripped down her cheek. It was her first day of marriage and already she was contemplating divorce. Brandy had been raised with the idea of permanency of marriage and had repeated the vows "until death do us part." But all along she had known in her heart that would not be the case. Reverend Rourke had known it also as he lifted his eyes to hers and made her repeat the words, phrase after phrase, slowly and solemnly.

It wouldn't do any good to cry over lost dreams. She had Eric to think about now, and that was problem enough without worrying over her silly romantic notions. She was exactly where she wanted to be, wasn't she? she thought. She had calmly and coldly linked her destiny—and Eric's—to Shaw Janus, at least for the time being. If she was going to force Shaw Janus to live up to the commitment she had tricked him into, she had to make the best of the situation—for everybody's sake.

Brandy sighed, wiping her high cheekbones with the back of her hand. She had a lot to do today even though she did not have a modeling session scheduled. She could not spend the day lolling about in bed like some honeymooning teenager. Even though her nineteenth birthday was several months away, Brandy felt she had passed into the world of adulthood; her childish dreams would stay forever locked in yesterday.

Brandy showered, washed her hair and stepped back into the clothes she had shed the night before. After

Shaw had fallen asleep, she had climbed into the bed beside him with the hope of presenting a picture of seduction in the morning. He had to believe he had made love to her so that she could use the consummation of their marriage as her one tenuous thread of keeping him bound to her. What little she had learned of him told her he was a man of mixed principles and she could only pray that those principles would extend to his feeling of obligation to her. She hoped he would feel guilty enough to want to do the "right thing" for her: to stay married long enough for her to obtain custody of Eric.

She put all of her cosmetics into her purse and picked up the paper he had left on the dresser. It was a copy of their blood test. Holding it now she could feel the same sense of surprise Shaw had felt when the reality of their situation washed over him. It shocked her, too. This long shot of maneuvering a man into marriage—Shaw Janus at that—was still a little difficult to comprehend. It would change her entire life, not just for the next few months, but for the rest of her life. Although she might want to deny it, she was Shaw Janus's wife. Someday she would be his ex-wife, but she would never be Brandy Logan again.

The thought made her sad, and she sat down on the edge of the bed to try to understand why. If this marriage was an intrusion to her life, she could imagine the obstacles it would present for Shaw. At least she had had time to think about it, to weigh the odds, to choose him. He, poor man, had been the victim, like it or not. And she had gotten him so drunk last night he had not even been able to consciously make a choice about the situation. But if she simply had gone to him, explained her problem, and asked him to marry her, purely on a business relationship, he would have refused. She had been forced to be devious. Thus she felt obligated to make life as simple as possible for him during their time together. She prayed he would agree to stay married to her for awhile.

Brandy thought back to the first time she had seen him, dressed to the nines in a vested suit with a tweedy trench coat. He looked like something out of an advertisement for men's clothing—one of the entirely untouchable higher echelon of males. For all the rumors of his carousing, he had seemed incongruously above the typical male image. He was, in fact, selective.

One night, while she had sat in the corner of his restaurant, she had watched three women approach him. She had almost held her breath wondering how he would respond. The women were very beautiful, by her estimation, in face as well as body, yet he seemed only amused by their performance.

He had bought them drinks, danced with them, sneaked kisses in the dusky light. But he had gone home from the supper club alone, obviously to the great disappointment of the three women.

She had witnessed the charm Shaw Janus could pour on for a female—if he wanted to, and Brandy had taken advantage of that. Fortunately, he also could not hold his liquor well.

She had watched him for a week, cataloging his tastes and habits. He drank Scotch with pretzels. He preferred blondes to brunettes, which, as a brunette, had worried her. He arrived alone and left alone, but she suspected he often made arrangements to meet someone elsewhere later: she had rarely observed him in his apartment late at night. Perhaps most curious of all, he continually took notes—on napkins which he would stuff into his jacket pockets, or on a notebook he sometimes carried with him. Once, she had even seen him make a notation on his hand.

Now she was married to Shaw Janus, had the key to his apartment and would see him there this evening.

Brandy considered going to her apartment, packing all the belongings she could manage in one trip and distributing them throughout his place, but second thoughts told her that would irritate him. She had him where she wanted him; she had to be tactful, meek and subservient in order to keep him there.

The first thing to do was convince him of the urgency of the situation. She had to make him see the importance of having Eric with her. Then she could worry about moving in with him—if he would let her.

Brandy went by her apartment to check her messages and change clothes. Her agent had not called, which meant she'd have no work again tomorrow, plus the added worry of whether she would have enough money on hand when the rent became due.

She took the time to select the most attractive outfit she owned—a pair of black velvet pants topped with a lacy pleated blouse with a black velvet tie at the throat. The effect was feminine, yet not too obvious, and understated, yet flattering.

Eric had spent the last few nights with a friend, and she had intended to let him stay in that comfortable routine until she could sort things out with Shaw. As she tried to think of ways to win Shaw's support, she thought of Eric. If only Shaw could love Eric as she did, he might want to help her keep him. Perhaps Eric himself could win Shaw over.

Brandy picked Eric up from school, collected some of his favorite playthings—a coloring book, a brand new box of crayons and a cigar box full of miniature dinosaurs—and drove over to Shaw's apartment.

"Whose house is this, Brandy?" Eric asked as he stood awed by the wide windows and sweeping view of the Atlanta skyline. Sunlight streamed in to the room full of luxurious furniture. There was not a magazine out of place on the low end tables, and not a cushion unfluffed on the huge sectional sofa that dominated the room. In the cases lining the wall, the books stood perfectly aligned next to a collection of knickknacks that were fortunately out of Eric's reach.

"It belongs to Mr. Janus," she whispered, afraid Shaw might emerge from the next room any moment and find them trespassing. The deep pile carpet was so soft beneath her feet that it revealed every step she took across the space.

"Who's he?" Eric whispered back, clutching his coloring book as if it were a security blanket.

"He's a very nice man," she said, hoping that would prove to be true. "He might let us live with him for awhile if we're very nice to him."

"But I don't want to live with him," Eric pleaded. "I want to live with you."

"Darling, I want that too." Brandy smiled, bending down to his level and hugging him, coloring book and all. "But I can't stay with you unless someone like Mr. Janus will let us live here together. Do you understand?"

He shook his head up and down, but was clearly

confused. She wondered how to explain the legalities of a situation to the child when she couldn't make sense of them herself.

"If Mr. Janus won't let us live with him, then you'll have to live with Aunt May and Uncle Louis."

"But I don't like them," Eric cried.

"I know, honey, but they like you. And they have lots of children for you to play with," Brandy explained patiently.

"I want to play with you."

"I know, sweetheart, and I want that too. But I can't stay with you by myself. I can only stay with you if someone like Mr. Janus will let us live with him."

"Then make him let us live here," Eric said.

Brandy chuckled at his simplicity. If only she could make Shaw understand their plight so easily. "I can't make him do that," she frowned, trying not to promise something she wasn't certain of herself. "I can only try to make him like us, and you must be very good to him so that he *will* like us and want us to stay with him."

"But I don't like him," Eric muttered.

"Sweetheart," she laughed, "you haven't even met him. He's a very nice man, I promise."

Eric looked so frightened and alone, even within the circle of her arms. She wanted to hold him closer and convince him they would always be together, but she knew she shouldn't. Their fate lay in Shaw Janus's hands. She couldn't resist Eric's frightened look; she hoped Shaw wouldn't be able to either.

It was close to seven o'clock when Brandy heard Shaw at the door. She had gone earlier to pick up Chinese food for dinner, hoping that Shaw liked it, and she had kept the dishes warming in the oven for over an hour. Eric had eaten earlier and was lying, chin in hands, in front of Shaw's wide-screen television set.

Even though she had been listening for him since five o'clock thinking he might get away early and hurry home to talk things out with her, Brandy's body jolted in panic when she heard the doorbell. It had to be Shaw, since she had the key to the apartment. How could she persuade him she needed his help? How could she hide her fear of losing Eric?

"Turn off the TV," she said to Eric who had looked up at her at the sound of the bell, "and go see who's there."

"Do I have to?" he whined.

"Please, Eric," her eyes pleaded, "and be very polite, okay?"

Even Eric could not resist Brandy's look. "Okay," he said, as he stood up, dusted off his pants as he had seen grownups do, and marched to the front door.

Brandy held her breath and leaned back against the cushions of the couch, positioned so that she could see Shaw's reaction as Eric opened the door.

He looked no more pleasant than he had when he left Brandy that morning. In fact, he seemed angrier. A scowl creased his brows, then disappeared as he realized someone much, much shorter than the woman he had expected was standing in front of him, only as tall as his knees. Shaw frowned, stepped back, then registered surprise as Eric greeted him as if it were Eric's home rather than his own.

"Hello, sir. My name's Eric. Do you want to see Brandy?"

Shaw stared down at Eric.

"What's your name?" said Eric, still holding the door politely, yet not inviting Shaw in.

"Shaw," he grumbled, "and yes, I do want to see Brandy." He looked into the room then, and nearly stabbed her with his eyes. "May I come in?" he addressed her.

"Invite Mr. Janus in, Eric."

"Please come in, sir." Eric opened the door wider with a great flourish, then waited until Shaw entered before closing it behind him.

Brandy stood, silently praying her knees wouldn't buckle beneath her. She had to give the impression of being strong, even though she didn't feel it. "I thought you'd be here earlier." She forced a smile, and ruffled Eric's hair as he came to stand beside her.

"I was busy," he snapped.

"Of course," she said demurely, thinking she knew what sort of activities usually kept him so busy.

"And I can't exactly say I was looking forward to coming home tonight," he added.

"No." She glanced swiftly up at him before returning her attention to Eric's mussed hair. "I can certainly understand how you feel."

"Can you now?" His eyes challenged her to meet him directly.

She mustered a bright smile. "Are you hungry?"

"Hungry?" he shrieked. Then he whispered somewhat more civilly as Eric looked up quickly at his exclamation. "Food is the furthest thing from my mind right now. We have some business to discuss, which I hope we can manage *alone*."

"I didn't think you'd get a chance to eat," she said, avoiding his eyes and his presence by stepping toward the kitchen, as far as possible away from him, "so I have a meal. It's always better to discuss things after you've had something nourishing."

"I do own a restaurant, you know. You shouldn't have gone to any trouble." He smiled, for Eric's benefit.

"Oh, it was no trouble," she hastened to assure him, going into the kitchen to escape him as well as to check that the food was not sticking to the pots or burning to a crisp.

Eric followed her, with Shaw right behind him.

"It's Chinese." Brandy unnecessarily stirred one of the concoctions. "Do you like Chinese?"

"Never touch the stuff."

"Why not?" She peeked into the oven and turned off the dials.

"I'm a meat and potatoes man, but there's no reason you should know that, nor any reason to concern yourself with that knowledge in the future," he asserted.

"I bet you've never eaten Chinese food," Brandy said, turning a sob into a laugh. So far he held all the cards and he was not dealing any to her.

"Never wanted to," Shaw said curtly.

"Oh, then let me fix a plate for you," she offered, "just to taste. You might find you'll really like it. I bought a variety."

Shaw leaned back against the doorjamb, crossed his arms over his broad chest and smiled. "Don't tell me you didn't cook all of this yourself? I'm disappointed."

"Don't be. I can cook, if that's what you're implying. But I thought this would be easier tonight since, as you said, we have so much to discuss."

Shaw looked from her to Eric, and back again. Eric just stared at him. "Did you bring any toys with you?" Shaw asked him.

"Yes, sir," Eric whispered, stepping back to clutch Brandy's pants' leg.

His quivering lower lip warned Brandy that tears were near. She knelt down beside Eric and gave him a big hug. *If only there were someone to reach out and give me some courage with a hug,* she thought.

"Why don't you go back into the living room and finish watching that show on TV? And you know what?" she prompted.

"What?" His eyes were nearly puddles of tears.

"Your favorite show comes on tonight."

"Which one?"

Brandy laughed. It hurt so much to love him. "The funny one with the animals," she said giggling.

"Really?"

"Promise." She nodded.

A quivering smile reached his lips as she held him away from her. "Now go on. I'll be right in here, and if you get hungry later, maybe we'll get some ice cream and cookies. Okay?"

He nodded solemnly, kissed her cheek and threw his arms around her neck. "I love you, Brandy."

"Oh, I love you too," she said and hugged him tightly. *Please let me keep Eric,* she silently prayed, then pushed him gently in the direction of the living room.

"Very touching," Shaw said when Eric was out of earshot.

Brandy stirred the Chinese vegetables vigorously, hoping the sound of the spoon scraping the pot would hide her sniffling. "Why?" she rounded on him, "because I love him? Because it's genuine, and not some delusion of caring simply for what you can get without giving of yourself? He's all I have, Shaw."

He seemed prepared with a retort, then thought better of it. "This has been quite a little show you've put on for me." He advanced into the kitchen, overseeing the collection of pots and pans on the stove, and the table set for two with bright napkins and gleaming cutlery. "The happy homemaker: a meal waiting on the table, a warm body busy at the stove and a child to make the family unit complete."

"It's not like that at all," she protested.

"Isn't it?"

"I was just trying to make things easier for you."

"After you've made them so difficult by sewing up my life in a neat little package? Instant wife and child without my consent," he countered.

"I had your consent."

"Not consciously." He glared at her.

"I'm trying to make you understand—"

"Don't," he cut her off. "*You* understand *me* for a change. I don't want a wife. I don't want a child, especially not someone else's. And I definitely do not want marriage, not even to someone as beautiful as you. I do not like package deals."

"But I—"

"Yes?" He waited patiently, without moving, and so quietly they could both hear the clock on the wall ticking.

"I need you, Shaw," she admitted.

He continued to stare at her for a very long moment. This time it was he who looked away first.

Brandy stood, shoulders drooping, at the stove. For her it was as simple as that. She needed him. She couldn't push him any more than she had already; he was the one to control the situation. She could talk until she was blue in the face, but he probably did not want to be reasoned with. She could beg and plead and scream, but it would do no good unless he was at least receptive to her problems. She had already accomplished the ultimate: trapping him in a marriage of *her* making. Now, if she remained here, it had to be at Shaw's invitation. He had every right to remove Brandy and Eric from his life.

The last few weeks flashed through her mind—all the efforts to keep Eric, all the frantic worry of finding a husband in a town where she barely knew any men. She had acted quickly in seeking support from a relative stranger, but at the time it had made sense and seemed the only solution. Maybe it hadn't been the right thing to do after all. Maybe she should just give up and let Louis and May take him.

"I am sorry," she swallowed, "for trying to manipulate you."

"What?" Shaw looked up at the sound of her mumbling.

"I apologize," she cleared her throat and spoke louder, "for involving you, Shaw. I guess I saw myself as some sort of savior for Eric, and it was wrong of me to play with your life. I don't think I really considered your feelings. I simply manufactured your reactions to follow my way of thinking. You have every right to be disgusted with me, and to resent everything I've engineered." She clutched the counter top behind her. "I had no business trying to control your life. I do badly enough with my own."

She couldn't look at him. She was afraid to see his wrath. "I won't fight you. I don't know how. I know someone who can undo this marriage probably a lot faster than it took to put it together."

Still he didn't respond, and she looked at him, eyes shining, and whispered, "I'm sorry."

The anger was gone from his face, as was all other emotion. He seemed puzzled, his eyes searching as he admitted, "I have to say I'm impressed."

"Please don't be sarcastic." She put her hands to her face, letting her hair fall forward to hide her tears. "I meant what I said just now. It's not some kind of ploy to gain your sympathy. I don't know you well enough to know how to appeal to you."

"I wasn't being sarcastic." He pulled out a chair from the table and sat down. "I am impressed. Impressed that you had the courage or determination or whatever to get me to marry you. Maybe you don't realize what an impossible feat that was."

Brandy took a deep breath, willing the tears to stop dripping from her eyes.

"Come sit down," he invited, "and we'll talk sensibly. Maybe I can help."

Warily, she approached the table and sank into the chair he had pulled out for her. She sniffed loudly. She wiped her hands across her cheeks to smear the tears away.

"You know, you're beautiful," he said, mesmerized by her simplest action, "even when you're crying." Realizing from the blush on her face what he had said, he coughed, wiggled in his chair, and got down to business. "I checked it out."

"Checked what out?"

"This marriage, and it is real, like it or not."

"I told you that this morning," she whispered, idly tracing a swirl in the woodgrain tabletop.

"You have to realize you gave me a rude awakening this morning with the news that I had actually married somebody. It wouldn't have mattered who it was. The fact of marriage just isn't the easiest thing for me to swallow."

"Yes, I do realize that now, and it was wrong of me to involve you."

He reached out and touched a strand of her dark, curling hair. "You did it for the best of reasons. I see that now."

"But I had no right—"

"No, you didn't. But I can't blame you for it totally. I mean, I must have cooperated to some extent, even if I don't remember doing it."

"You did," she whispered. "No one said the words for you. It wasn't a marriage by proxy."

"Well, there then." He smiled and shook his head. "Then I asked for it." He raised his eyes questioning, "Why did I ask for it? Oh, never mind." He looked back at her. "The fact is we are married, for better or worse. Now we need to decide what to do about it."

"We'll get an annulment, of course. It's the easiest way out for you."

"But not for you."

Brandy looked at him, surprised at the sincerity in his eyes. She shook her head.

"What is it that you're actually asking of me?" Shaw prompted. "Come on," he coaxed when she continued to trace the woodgrain lines. "If I understand exactly what you need, maybe I can help in some way. You did want my help, didn't you?"

She nodded. "But you can't help unless you're my husband. I'm underage, you see, and the courts don't want to put Eric in my custody. I don't represent the stable home environment he needs. I work. I'm a model. I can't be home when he gets in from school. I can't be a mother to him they say, much less a father. They think since I'm single and supposed to be always concerned with dating, that I won't be home for Eric in the evenings, either. And financially, well, I'm not making that much now, and I guess that part frightens me most, because I can barely support myself. But one day soon, I just feel it, I'm going to be Atlanta's top model. Then, maybe I'll even go to New York."

His eyes looked fierce when she glanced at him, like a cat ready to pounce, she thought, and she noticed that his eyes were green.

"I'm beginning to get the picture," he said, "but why me? Wasn't there anyone else you could have married? A boyfriend? Someone you might have known from school?"

Brandy shook her head. "I haven't made many friends since I moved to Atlanta. I've been too busy trying to work, and the men I meet are either married or utter creeps. I always have to fight them off—"

"Fight them off? What do you mean?" he asked sharply.

"I'm exaggerating, I guess. It's only happened once or twice."

He frowned and his voice became gruff. "Explain."

"Well, I was modeling this practically sheer teddy one day and the photographer—"

"Ugh," he groaned. "Don't tell me any more. I can guess. Well, you asked for it, you know."

"I did not!" she wailed. "My agent sent me over there. He doesn't get many calls for short girls like me, so I have to take every job he sends me if I want to eat. And I was just trying to do my job. I wasn't trying to . . . to . . ."

He looked at her, shaking his head. "Spare me. Well, what about someone from back home? Where do you come from?"

"Bainbridge. It's a little town."

"I know what it is. Weren't there any available men there you could have married?"

"I wasn't very popular in school, and I didn't know many boys." It wouldn't serve any purpose to explain how sheltered her upbringing had been, how she'd had only one date during all of high school. His eyes said he found her words hard enough to believe.

"If I'd been in that school, you would have been my private property and I'd be fighting to keep the wolves away from you."

"It wasn't like that at all," she explained, "I was very shy. And I was too busy trying to finish school a year early so that I could move away. I hated living there. You see, I lived with Louis and May, so I know what it's like. And I don't want that for Eric."

Shaw slid his chair back and stretched his long legs in front of him. "I'm beginning to see."

"So what happens now?"

Shaw shrugged. "I need to think."

She nodded, rearranging the place setting she had meticulously set for their meal. "Are you hungry? We could be eating while you're thinking."

He shrugged again and she took that as a sign to ladle out the food. Anything to keep busy, to stop her mind for a few moments. Brandy picked up the two plates and carried them to the stove, unaware that Shaw was watching every move she made.

"I brewed some hot tea," she said over her shoulder. "That's traditional for Chinese food, but if you'd like something else, I'll get it for you."

"Wouldn't want to break tradition now, would we?" he grimaced. "What is all this stuff?" He stared at the conglomeration on his plate.

Brandy told him the names of the various dishes she had selected: subgum chicken, wontons and spareribs.

"Not bad." He crunched down on a water chestnut. "Not as exotic as it sounds."

Brandy half-smiled, and ate in silence. "More tea?" She filled his cup, wondering what her fate would be.

Shaw got up for a second helping before she could even offer, refilling his plate and asking if he could do the same for her.

"We'll have to have this more often," he said, chasing a snow pea onto his fork.

"We?" Brandy looked up.

Shaw shrugged. "You might not be so bad to have around—for awhile."

Brandy held her breath. Could he mean that?

Chapter Three

Brandy sat across from Shaw Janus, watching as he ate his second helping of Chinese food. He looked so domestic, so very much the part she had gambled he could play. Had she glimpsed this side of him during those nights she watched him in the restaurant? Was this why she had been so determined to "trap" him? Had she married him for her own selfish reasons? No, that wasn't quite true. She had done it all for Eric's sake.

Shaw looked so different now: shirt unbuttoned, tie askew, shoes off under the table, a lock of recalcitrant hair at his forehead—all signs of his being comfortable at home. He could be comfortable, she reminded herself, since he was home. *She* was the one who was the stranger, even if she was married to him.

She wondered why she had pursued him so relentlessly the previous week. What had made her think she could make him care about a perfect stranger—*two* strangers for that matter? Why had she clung to the hope of salvation with him against all odds? He was right. If she had simply needed a husband, there were other men she could have asked outright to marry her and not have to play this charade.

She couldn't have married any of them. Barry was too boring. She would never be able to adjust to his interest in mechanics. She hated drag racing, and couldn't imagine spending the rest of her life, or at least the next few weeks, listening to him talk about "souped up" cars and "fast changes in the pits."

Eugene? He cared—about her body, and that was all. His heart, if he had one, was in the wrong place.

But hadn't she used *her* body, *her* looks, to trap Shaw? Hadn't she counted on her sex appeal to trap him into marrying her? Was there a difference?

Compassion had made the difference. It was in his eyes, in those tiny lines around the corners that spoke of laughter, loving, caring. She must have seen it to have pursued him so relentlessly.

Eugene's eyes had no other look but desire.

And there was Carl. He would have married her, but she couldn't even begin to ask him. It would be too much of a burden for him. He was just beginning to establish himself in the business world. The expense of a wife and instant child would have been a strain on him. Besides, he had never been able to accept her wanting Eric, and would eventually resent her for interfering with his career plans.

Yet, she had thrust herself into Shaw's life and interrupted whatever plans he might have for the future.

Compassion, she thought, smiling briefly as he caught her staring at him. She returned her attention to the food on her plate, thinking, *it's in his eyes. It's what I need from him, and what I'm counting on.*

But all too late she was realizing she didn't have the right to manipulate his life. She had to let go and let fate work out her future and Eric's without involving Shaw. It would be worse for her to try to keep Eric if fate had something better in mind for them.

"Shaw," she whispered, "I really am sorry I forced myself on you, into your life. It was wrong, and you have every right to feel angry."

"I'll get used to it." He continued eating.

Brandy looked across at him, searching for the truth in his eyes, but he kept them averted.

"I—I guess I was just desperate. I felt so alone and helpless, and somehow you popped up on the scene and the more I thought of you, the more it made sense to reach out to you. But I went about it all the wrong way. I should have approached you directly."

"Wouldn't have worked," he munched, swallowing his words.

"No, not anymore than it is now."

"Now that's where you're wrong." He held out his cup for more tea.

Brandy poured in silence. She'd missed something in the exchange.

"How?"

"If you had approached me openly, appealing to me with your problem of being fatherless, I would have thought, 'Hey, this kid's in trouble. She really needs help. But not from me. No sir, not me.' Instead, you sized me up, however correctly or incorrectly, decided I was the answer to your problem, and you involved me," he explained, "and now I am part of your problem, like it or not."

"Yes, but it was wrong, what I did. It can be undone."

Shaw set his tea cup on the saucer, placed his fork on his plate, and turned to Brandy. "Do you believe in fate? Destiny? Kismet?"

Brandy shrugged. "I suppose so."

"Then you have to believe that this was meant to be, this psuedo-marriage between us. Even if I'd known what you were planning, I couldn't have gotten out of it. It was destined. I don't know why—I know why you needed to get married," he clarified his statement, "but I haven't figured out why I was supposed to be the one you married. I guess that will come in time, but for right now, like it or not, I accept it."

"You do?"

"Obviously not very gracefully. I'm still trying to adjust to the idea. But yes, I do accept it. We were meant to be together, for that child's sake, if for nothing else."

"You really think so?"

He lifted his eyes heavenward. "I hope so. Otherwise, none of this makes the slightest bit of sense."

"But—"

"But what?"

"You—you don't mind?"

"Mind?" He raised his voice and shoved back his plate. "I mind like hell! But that's my problem. I'll deal with it. Give me a chance, will you? I'm still trying to accept the fact that I'm married. That's a real mind-bender."

Brandy sat silently, wondering what to say and what to do. Shaw had the upper hand; she was at his mercy. "What do you want me to do?" she asked.

"I don't know." He shook his head. "I'm still trying to think the whole thing through. We need to backtrack a little, to go back to square one. I still hardly know who you are. Yet you're married to me."

"Well, my name is—"

"I know, Brandy Logan. You're thinking of keeping your maiden name for professional reasons. You're a model, and you're eighteen. I do remember that from this morning."

"Then what would you like to know?"

"I don't know right now. I need some space. I still have a lot of thinking to do."

Shaw thrust back his chair and stalked away from the table. Brandy opened her mouth to say something, then shut it again. His anger seemed to be simmering just below the surface and she didn't want to do anything to provoke him into a violent eruption. He paced up and down in the small space of the kitchen. Brandy chewed at her fingernails, but not hard enough to break them. She needed to keep them long and shapely for photographs.

"Maybe it would be better for you if Eric and I left now," she mumbled.

"What?"

"I said, I think Eric and I will go home . . . to let you think."

"Home?" He chuckled. "You are home. Or didn't you mean it when you said you needed a husband?

Most husbands and wives—loving ones, that is—live under the same roof."

"Yes, of course, but—"

"We might as well go all the way with this little picture of suburban existence so the judge believes it, don't you agree?"

Brandy sighed knowing he was right, but not certain what actually living with Shaw Janus would involve. "I'll have to go home tonight, though," she said.

"Why?"

"I didn't bring anything with us," she explained. "I wasn't certain you were going to let us stay."

"If I'm going to have a wife," Shaw smiled, pausing long enough to think about the specifics of the arrangement, "she's going to live in. It wasn't so bad coming home tonight to a meal all laid out on the table. I could get used to that . . . and other things."

Brandy quickly caught on to his line of thinking, speaking hastily to avoid the issue that was really bothering her—how to keep him out of her bed. "I love to cook, when I have time. I'll be glad to have meals ready for you, when I can, but I work, too, you know, sometimes until very late at night, and often don't even have time for more than a nutrition bar during the day."

"No wonder you're so thin." His eyes roamed over her body.

"But you don't come home for meals every night, do you? I mean, I didn't think you ever ate at home."

His brows went up. "I could be tempted to change some of my habits. Not all, mind you, but some. And let's get one thing straight right now. Just because you got me to be your husband for however long that might be, don't think you can make me into the model husband. I don't expect to change my whole life because of you."

Brandy blushed. She already had some idea of the number of women he must have listed in his little black book. "I know." She buried her face beneath the fall of her dark curls. She couldn't understand how a man could juggle several women at once. She never would. It would always be one man for her, even now. They might not be a true couple, but they were married, and she intended to be faithful to that position.

"Well," Shaw said, disconcerted that she hadn't given him the argument he had been expecting, "as long as we have that clear, we might as well move you in here."

Brandy still hadn't adjusted to the idea of actually living with a man. She had maintained her virginity on their wedding night, but he wasn't aware of that. Worse was the question of whether or not she would be able to maintain that position tonight, when he was thinking clearly, and standing tall and strong in front of her. Yet, could she deny him that right without getting into an argument with him? She had to think of something, some way to keep him out of her bed. It would not be easy with only two bedrooms in the apartment, and Eric sleeping in one of them. After she had demanded so much of Shaw, he was in a position to make his own demands on her.

"I—I'll wash the dishes when we come back," she mumbled. That would at least give her some time to stall, she thought, and maybe she would think of something by then. If only they could be civil about the whole thing—he take one room, she and Eric the other. But somehow Shaw didn't look the type to ignore a woman physically, particularly when he could rightfully claim her as his wife.

"Right, let's go then," Shaw said.

"Eric and I can manage on our own," she offered, "if you have something else you'd like to do. I don't want to change your life any more than you say you'll allow it changed."

"I'm not a total heel, you know," he said with annoyance, "and I don't like the idea of someone like you out alone on the streets at night."

"What do you mean, someone like me?"

He lifted his eyes to the ceiling. "You are naive. You must know how beautiful you are, and driving alone with a little boy at this hour of the night could be dangerous."

"It's not late."

"It's dark."

"But it's only dark because there's a storm brewing. I do it all the time."

"Not anymore, if I can help it."

"Why not?"

"Because a lot can happen in this city—in any city, for that matter. And I don't like to see any woman out alone, if that makes you feel any better," he retorted.

She didn't think it did, but she nodded anyway. They'd be having a real argument soon enough. No sense in precipitating it over whether or not he would accompany her to her apartment. She would like some help carrying things, and had to admit she'd never liked being out alone at night even back in Bainbridge. "I'll get my purse," she assented.

She was silent on the drive to her apartment, speaking just to give him directions. Eric, sensing the tension, clutched her hand as he sat in the seat between the two of them. An unsettling frown marred his forehead, but he was either too shy or frightened of Shaw to ask Brandy questions in front of him. Brandy would try to explain it all to him later as well as she could.

"The house on the hill," Brandy directed.

Shaw pulled up to the curb. "Nice neighborhood, but expensive. I didn't realize models made so much money," he commented.

"They don't. I have a little apartment in one part of the house. It was the cheapest thing I could find in a convenient location." She hoped he wouldn't make much comment about the sparsity of her furnishings. It took nearly all she had just to keep up the rent.

Brandy handed him the key and held her breath to wait for his reaction.

The front room was practically wall-to-wall with plants surrounding two beanbag chairs Brandy had made herself. It looked comfortable, but quite a contrast to Shaw's living room.

"If I were a grasshopper I'd feel right at home here," he muttered, moving through to the next room where stood Brandy's bed, which consisted of a mattress and box spring on a frame. She couldn't afford matching furniture or a headboard, but the sheets were colorful.

She had found an old bureau in a secondhand furniture store. The leg was loose and she had to be careful whenever she moved it, but she had stripped it and antiqued it in a cream color to blend with the earth tones of the sheets. A brick and board bookcase stood against the opposite wall.

"Read a lot, do you?" Shaw raised his brows, somewhat skeptically.

"Yes, I do," Brandy stated, unwilling to admit she

was also hoping to go back to night school to earn a college degree as soon as she had enough money.

He didn't look into the bathroom, which contained more plants. It was the only "furniture" she had acquired with little expense, people giving her cuttings and chipped pots, and had become a hobby for her.

There was no furniture in the kitchen, but she had plenty of dishes.

"I was wondering," Brandy began.

"Yes?"

"If I should keep my apartment during our, uh, temporary arrangement. It was so hard to find. There were three people standing on the doorstep waiting to snatch it up right after me."

"That would be a stupid waste of money," Shaw said, surveying the kitchen with his hands on his hips, "and from the looks of things, you could use the money more wisely elsewhere."

"But it would be somewhere I could go to get out of your hair, if you want the apartment free." She blushed.

"It might not be a bad idea for me to keep your apartment." He pursed his lips.

"Oh, no, I don't think so," she hesitated. The idea of her apartment, her furnishings, her bed being used by someone else disturbed her. "Maybe I should get rid of it. I was wondering how I'd explain my absence to my landlady anyway."

"Right. Let's get started then. Just take what you think you'll need tonight and I'll get the rest this weekend. We can probably store the bed somewhere at the office. That looks like the biggest problem. And do you have to keep all these plants?"

"Oh, yes!" She almost cried at the thought of losing

them, then realized what an inconvenience this verita-
ble plant shop was going to be for him, imposed in with
his sophisticated decor. "Please?"

Shaw nodded, not even attempting to talk her out of
it. He seemed to realize these few plants and posses-
sions were all she owned in the world. "Why don't I
start packing up your dishes while you get the things
you need? Do you have any cardboard cartons?"

"No, but my landlady probably does. Shall I go ask
her for some?"

"I'll go," Eric piped up.

The sound of his small voice when he had been so
silent on the drive over, even when asked questions
about his age and his school, caused Shaw to turn and
stare. "Oh, so you do have a voice after all?" Shaw
grinned.

Eric hung his head and ran to Brandy, clutching at
her hand.

"A momma's boy, too," commented Shaw under his
breath, then a bit more loudly, "rather an auntie's
boy."

"He's just shy around strangers." Brandy glared.
"You would be too if you'd been through all he has in
the last few weeks. And now having to leave here and
move in with you. You have to admit that's unsettling
for anyone. I'm not exactly looking forward to it
myself."

"Nor am I." Shaw's eyes glowered at her.

Brandy hung her head. "I'm sorry. Of course you
aren't. But it's no reason to take out your frustrations
on Eric. Can't you give him a chance? Give us both a
chance? You might find we're not such bad company."

"I suppose I'll have to." His lips were set in an
uncompromising slit. "Now, about those boxes."

"I'll go," Eric said again.

"My, but you are eager to get those cartons, aren't you?" Shaw grinned for Eric's benefit, but Brandy could tell he was still angry.

"He likes to play with Mrs. McGinty's dog," Brandy explained.

"She has a dog?" Shaw encouraged Eric to talk. "What's his name?"

"It's a she dog," Eric replied, "and she's a dachshund, and her name is Pepper. Pepper's fun, unless you pull her tail. She doesn't like that at all. She snapped at me the time I did it, and I wouldn't ever do it again. Mrs. McGinty said I shouldn't."

"Smart man." Shaw smiled, and this time Brandy felt it was more genuine. He walked over to where Eric stood clutching Brandy's hand and stooped down to his level. "But don't you think that if Mrs. McGinty has some cartons we can borrow that they might be too big for you to carry?"

"I suppose so," Eric replied, hanging his head again as if he had just been reprimanded for pulling Pepper's tail.

"Then why don't we both go?" Shaw suggested. "I might need someone to play with Pepper so that she doesn't accidentally get underfoot when I carry out those boxes."

"That's a good idea." Eric's face lit up and he held out his hand to Shaw. "I'll show you the way."

Shaw glared over Eric's head at Brandy and taking Eric's outstretched hand in his large palm, he stood. "Lead the way, my man."

"Is it okay, Brandy?" Eric asked, looking back at her.

"Of course it is." She smiled, watching them go out

the back screen door, but she was having second thoughts. What would Shaw tell Mrs. McGinty about the move? She should have been the one to tell her landlady herself. She was almost like a mother to her. But what could she tell the woman? She had just paid the rent, so there would be no problem with that. She would have to explain to Mrs. McGinty somehow, but as she turned to pack her suitcases and Eric's, she knew she did not feel up to it that night. She only hoped Shaw would know best how to deal with the explanations. She was after all, at least where Eric was concerned, relying heavily on his control of the situation.

Although Brandy had lived in the apartment for a short time, she was sorry to leave it. It held a few good memories, and she'd miss her house neighbor who had added so extensively to her store of house plants.

Then, there was the evening that Carl had told her he loved her. It was a poignant scene, still vivid and bittersweet because it was the first time a man had professed love for her. She had almost wanted to tell him she loved him, too, but she hadn't.

Perhaps love was just not meant to happen to her. Her marriage to Shaw would certainly postpone it for a long time. She felt suddenly as trapped as Shaw must be feeling.

Two cartons edged their way through the doorway, followed by Eric and a yapping Pepper, who raced up to Brandy for the customary pat on the head.

"She has more if we need them," Shaw announced, sliding the boxes across the countertop in the kitchen. "Need any help with your packing?"

"Will those boxes fit in your car?"

"No." Shaw started stacking dishes into the nearest one. "I'll have to rent or borrow a truck."

"I'm sorry."

"Don't keep apologizing." He clattered the crockery in his haste. "It's not going to help now."

"What did you tell her?" she asked.

"Who? Your landlady?" He looked up just in time to catch her nod. "The truth—that you swept me off my feet, and in a fit of mental incapacity married me, and we're going to live happily ever after at my place . . . at least until the divorce."

"You didn't tell her that, did you?"

"Of course not, but I should have. She's a nice lady . . . very upset at your sudden move."

Brandy sighed. "I guess I realized she would be. I'll talk to her when we come back."

"I took the liberty of assuring her you would. I told her, in fact, that you were so upset at the idea of leaving such a fine home and landlady that you sent me over tonight for the boxes."

He could charm the skin off a snake if he put his mind to it, thought Brandy. How in the world had she ever managed to get him married to her? "Thank you," she whispered. "I do feel that way."

"I know," he muttered, and Brandy realized that the compassion she had glimpsed was showing its head again. He was a man who cared about people. She only hoped he could come to care enough about her and Eric. She also hoped he didn't care too much to let her sleep alone tonight.

Chapter Four

The return drive seemed to take forever, and it didn't help matters when tubfuls of rain poured down from the sky. Shaw slowed the car to a crawl, straining to see the flooded streets between each brief swipe of the wipers.

"This weather is fit for Noah and the ark, not automobiles," Shaw muttered, the strain of driving showing in his white knuckles against the wheel and his intent concentration on the fogging windshield.

"I'm sorry I made you come out in this kind of weather," Brandy apologized, leaning forward as if she could help him drive by watching the road ahead. She was nervous enough dreading their arrival back at the apartment, not needing this delay of the expected confrontation.

"It's not your fault," he mumbled, then swore as a car in another lane splashed a blinding sheet of spray onto the car's hood. "You may be able to control some impossible feats, but the weather isn't one of them."

"What do you mean?" Brandy glanced briefly at him.

"I mean this marriage of ours." He shook his head. "I'm still not sure how you managed that."

She didn't answer immediately, and when she did, Shaw could barely hear her. "If it makes you feel any better, the shock of it is setting in with me, too."

Shaw didn't respond to that, so Brandy continued. "I suppose what I did is akin to people who develop extraordinary strengths when they're in trouble. You know, to lift cars and push impossible objects out of the way . . . sort of like a miracle."

"I wouldn't exactly describe our marriage in that light," Shaw retorted.

Brandy was afraid to ask how he would describe it, sure it would be unfit for Eric's ears, even though the boy was asleep between them on the front seat.

Last night, her wedding night, she had wondered how she would manage to survive. Tonight seemed worse. Tonight, Shaw was sober. There was nothing to stand between them but a sleeping six-year-old.

"I'm afraid this is as close as I can get to the building." Shaw drew the car up to the nearest curb.

"You'll get drenched." Brandy's eyes were wide with concern as Shaw waited for her to open the door and run with Eric to the lobby.

"It won't be the first time," he smiled, "and it will probably match my mood."

"Oh, well, thank you." She blushed, reaching behind the seat to pick up some of her belongings.

"Leave those." Shaw put his hand on her arm. "I'll get them later, if this lets up. You won't be needing too much anyway, not if last night was any indication."

She didn't think her face could turn any redder, but she felt it turn three degrees warmer. "Last night was the exception," she retorted. "Tonight, if I wore everything that's piled on the back seat of this car, it wouldn't be too much." She grabbed a handful of hangered clothes and was preparing to pull them over the front seat and out the door with her when his strong hand stopped her.

"Leave it, I said. I'll get it later."

Brandy glared at him, but could not bring herself to openly defy him after the look with which he challenged her. "Eric." She shook his shoulder. "Wake up. We have to run through the rain to the building. Are you awake, honey?"

He yawned and nodded.

"Take my hand, and run when I open the door." She smiled, hoping he would think this was a game. What a welcome to their new home—a mad dash through the downpour.

"Ready?" Shaw took up the spirit of a game, grinning, setting them on their mark and counting them down before he leaned across Brandy, deliberately holding his arm against her breasts just ever so much longer than necessary before shouting, "go," and flinging open their door.

Eric dashed in front of Brandy and splashed through the puddles to the door. Brandy, trying to hold up the hems of her velvet pants and knowing they would never be the same again, was blinded by her curly hair plastered to her face. One minute she was skipping across a wide depression in the sidewalk, and the next she was sprawled over it in an ungraceful heap with a sore rump.

"Brandy!" Shaw was shouting in her ear. "Are you all right?"

"I don't know." She caught her breath wondering how he could have gotten out of the car and to her side so quickly. "You've left the car door wide open."

"Damn the car door!" He bent over her, protecting her as much as he could from the rain with his body. "Can you move? Can you get up?"

"I think so. I hope so." *Oh, how embarrassing,* was her first thought. Then she wondered if this wasn't actually a lucky move. A man like Shaw would not want to make love to a hunchback, would he? "Oh," she moaned, "I ache all over."

"Have you broken anything?" he persisted, helping her stretch.

Eric held the door wide while Shaw carried Brandy through and deposited her on the nearest chair. He knelt in front of her and pushed her stringy hair out of her face. "Are you all right?"

"Most of me is." Her lips quivered on the verge of a smile to reassure him, but not enough to set his mind completely at ease. "It's just not too comfortable sitting down." She rubbed her shoulder. "Or moving."

"I'd better call a doctor."

"No, Shaw, that won't be necessary. Really, I'm probably just bruised . . . oh," she groaned.

"Where does it hurt?" he responded to her agonized moan.

"I just thought, a bruise is going to look terrific with a swimsuit."

"That we'll discuss later," he scowled. "Can I get you anything right now? Water? Aspirin?"

"I've had enough water, thank you, but an aspirin would be ambrosia. I can wait until we get to the apartment." She struggled to stand.

"Sit right back down there, lady." His hands forced her shoulder down.

"Ouch, that hurts." She twisted to look at her shoulder exposed by the torn seam of her sleeve. "Just a graze though, don't you think?"

"Nothing feels broken," he said, and gently probed her shoulder.

"Your car door's still open." She glanced through the door. "You've probably left the keys in the ignition. Anyone could steal the car."

"They'd be welcome to it at the moment." His eyes never left her. "But if you promise not to budge an inch, and I mean an inch, lady, I'll go finish parking the car and come back to take you upstairs."

"I'll stay put." Her eyes were wide with surprise that he should be so concerned about her. "I promise."

"I've heard you keep promises, at least for Eric," he commented. "I hope you will for me as well."

"Promises are very serious business with me," she answered.

"If I didn't know better," he stood up, hands on his hips, eyes puzzled as he stared at her, "I'd think you were enjoying this."

She frowned at him. "It did hurt. I mean, it still does, too." She added to herself, it might just be the excuse she needed to stay out of his bed. At least for another night. "You'd better go move your car."

"You stay put." He pointed his finger at her, then stood Eric in front of her. "Make sure she doesn't move, okay?"

Brandy had to admit her helplessness appeared more convincing with Shaw carrying her up to the apartment. Her heart was aching more, though, from the nearness of his body than from her bruises. He was soaked as she was, and where his arm contacted her back, cradling her against him, she felt absolutely naked. She permitted herself to groan for the sake of her appearance.

"Hang on." He hurried along the corridor, concerned with her recurring sounds of discomfort. "We're almost there. Try not to faint."

"I'm not going to faint."

"Good," he snapped. "Because you're heavy enough as it is without being a dead weight if you faint."

"Oh," she moaned again.

"Where does it hurt now?" He tried to juggle her and insert the key in the door at the same time.

"OW!" she complained genuinely this time as he swung around and her elbow slammed into the doorjamb. "You don't have to sling me about as if I were a sack of potatoes. I'd rather lie in a heap on your doorstep than be bashed to death against the walls."

"Sorry, but I'm not used to carrying people over my threshold. The instructions weren't included with my little black book. And how they managed the key in the lock with the girl in their arms in all those old movies I'll never know."

"Obviously," sarcasm edged her voice, "with someone as heavy as I am, especially for such a strong man as yourself, it probably took the aid of a winch."

"More than likely," he finally managed to kick the

door wider with Eric's help turning the key in the lock, "those Don Juans carried wenches with them."

"Don't get any ideas with me, Shaw Janus," she pouted at his pun.

"Ideas?" He laughed as if he were the villain in an old and very bad movie. "That's all I've had since I married you, wife . . . and I would guess similar thoughts have been circulating in your mind." Brandy gasped, but he quieted her with his next remark. "You even managed to get me to carry you over the threshold. You're turning me into a traditionalist!"

"Ow!" Brandy moaned in pain and frustration as he dumped her, wet clothes and all, onto his immaculate couch. "Oh, it really does hurt, but a lot you care!"

He stood back and surveyed her drenched frame, admiring the curving flesh all but exposed to his view. "I care enough to offer to help you undress."

Brandy's face flamed, her eyes darting to Eric hovering anxiously behind Shaw. "You'd better hurry out of those wet clothes," she spoke around Shaw's knees directly to Eric. "Take a warm bath and jump into bed."

"Excellent idea." Shaw turned to Eric, helping him unbutton his shirt. "Can you manage alone, Eric? Or do you need help?"

"I can do it by myself." Eric raised his chin to its highest position.

"And don't forget the teeth!" Brandy warned. "You have to brush his teeth after he finishes," she added for Shaw's benefit. "He misses places."

"Off to the bath with you then." Shaw nudged Eric's shoulder. "You can have the guest bathroom all to yourself."

Brandy smiled after Eric, watching him trudge off

like a man in control of his own destiny. "That's very nice of you to be so kind to Eric, Shaw. I'm sure you'll see he's really not any trouble at all."

"Glad to help out." He grinned, casting his eyes back in her direction. "Now, let's see what I can do with you. My bath's big enough for the two of us."

Brandy dragged her damaged frame into a more decorous position. "Wait a minute, Shaw. I think we need to get a few things clear."

"Do we now?" He inclined his ear. "I thought that was what we had done earlier. You needed a husband, I provided. It was your idea, after all, not mine."

"Yes, but—" She waved her hands, hoping he would fill in the blanks without her having to spell everything out. She had never discussed intimacies with a man before and she found it difficult to begin.

"I'm waiting."

"But all I needed was a husband to—to—be a father to Eric."

"A name you could write 'Mrs.' in front of? Someone whose name you could use to fill in the blank marked 'Who will pay this account?' Someone to provide a home for you and Eric?" he demanded.

"Yes, exactly."

"I'm perfectly willing to provide all of that for you, Brandy."

Brandy sighed. "Thank you."

"But the term 'husband' in my book also implies conjugal rights."

Brandy tried to sit up straighter, and the effort reminded her of how much she was depending on her injuries to keep her out of this kind of a situation. "Oh," she cried, "can't you see I'm in pain?"

"I don't believe in headaches." Shaw loomed over her.

"It's not my head that hurts!" Brandy lashed out at him, aware now that subtleties would bounce like a rubber ball off this man when he set his mind to something. "And as far as your conjugal rights are concerned, you can't possibly know what the true qualities of a husband are when you've enjoyed your conjugal rights without the benefit of marriage until now!"

"Can I help it if you made an honest man of me?"

"Let's get one thing straight, Shaw Janus! I am not going to share your bed! If you insist on keeping your bedroom privileges with other women, then you can forget about expecting the same with me."

"I had no idea you felt so strongly about the subject," he said.

"I do!" Brandy glared, sensing victory over Shaw.

He put his hand to his chin and was silent. Then he said quietly, "I guess you're worth giving up other women . . . for the duration of this marriage. You must be, or I wouldn't have made love to you in the first place last night."

Brandy blushed. He was too astute at turning the conversation to his favor. "I'm not interested," she said, as if she had any choice in a matter Shaw would decide on and carry out in spite of her objections. "Pleasure is all that interests you . . . and I won't be cold and ruthless about something that should be a warm and loving experience. Get your pleasure elsewhere!"

"Like you did last night?" he asked mockingly.

"That was different!"

"How? Because you got me drunk first?" He

laughed. "What a switch. Usually that works the other way around."

"I've already told you I regret the way things happened last night. I regret having involved you in my problems."

"Yet you needed me. And still do, if I'm not mistaken."

Brandy lifted her face, tears flooding her eyes and ready to spill down her cheeks. "That's true, but I won't be blackmailed into keeping you on our side. I've already offered you your freedom."

"After you stole it from me."

"I've admitted that. I've apologized. I've tried to make it up to you in the best way I can."

"This conversation seems to be going round in circles," he said, shaking his head, "while we're both dripping on the furniture and allowing pneumonia to set in. A hot bath and some warm clothes will make a big difference."

"I will not take a bath with you." She cringed as he bent forward to pick her up. "Like Eric, I'm perfectly capable of managing on my own."

"Maybe," he said softly, as he put his arms around her wriggling frame, "but I need someone to scrub my back."

"Don't touch me, Shaw Janus! You don't own me!"

"Don't I?" He held her gaze with his deep, piercing eyes. "You were in my bed this morning. I'm not asking for anything unreasonable, merely a repeat of what must have occurred last night."

Brandy was tempted to tell him nothing had happened, but if she did, he would have absolutely no moral reason to feel responsibility for her and Eric. His words made sense: it was her own doing that had put her in his arms. She just had to remember that it was all for Eric's sake. She might as well get used to the idea. It couldn't be that bad . . . but would she know what to do? Wouldn't he see through her sham immediately? How could she have allowed herself to be bewitched by his logic?

"Shaw, really, I can manage on my own." Brandy cringed back against the couch.

"Let it never be said I don't live up to my responsibilities." Shaw ignored her protests and placed his hands on each side of her face, trapping her with his eyes. "And one thing I cannot do is ignore a helpless woman, especially one who is in such pain."

"I'll make a quick recovery." Brandy tried to look anywhere but at his lips, hovering so close to her own. She wiggled as best she could in the confined area, and winced with the soreness that was beginning to set in. "Besides," she tried to look around him, "you haven't brought my clothes up. Why don't you go down to the car for them, and by the time you get back I'll be all finished in the bath? I'll even save you a lot of hot water."

"There's plenty of hot water," he said, his face so close to hers rain droplets fell from his hair onto her cheek, "and more than enough room for the two of us. Trust me."

"I suppose you're speaking from experience about the adequacies of the tub," her voice quivered.

Shaw neither confirmed nor denied it as his mouth descended on her own. "Don't fight me, Brandy," he mumbled against her lips. "You didn't last night."

"How do you know what I did last night?" She shook her face free of his lips, pounding ineffectually with her fists against his chest. "You were so drunk last night you probably don't remember a thing!"

"If I was drunk, it was your fault." He blazed. "I don't make a habit of drowning my senses in drink. But I suppose that was necessary for you to have your way with me, wasn't it? Wasn't it?" he demanded, scooping up both of her flailing hands in one of his.

Brandy couldn't deny it. Alcohol had contributed greatly to her success with him. It seemed there was no way she could fight him now—not with words, nor logic, nor compromise. Tears, she recalled from that morning, had not been such a winning ploy, either.

"You had your way with me last night," his voice could have frozen an ocean. "Now it's your turn to give me equal time."

As his lips came down on hers this time, Brandy found it not an unpleasant sensation—actually, it was very enjoyable. The pressure of his mouth on hers drew her into the spirit of his lovemaking, gently guiding and teasing her lips apart, inviting his questing tongue. Brandy had rarely been kissed before, and never like this. She felt weak and fluttery in her stomach, no longer concerned with the consequences of her actions. Shaw was her husband, legally and morally; there was nothing wrong in what they were doing, unless she wanted an annulment later. An end to the marriage was inevitable since Shaw didn't love her, but she wanted it to end with an annulment rather than a divorce.

But at that moment, she couldn't argue about it. It was too easy to just lay back and follow Shaw's lead.

"You're lovely," Shaw murmured, his hands framing her face, dropping down to the buttons of her blouse, "even when you're as wet as a half-drowned rat."

"You're wonderful for a girl's ego," she sighed, mesmerized by the action of his fingers at the closure of her blouse. The fluttery sensation drifted lower, until she was squirming with impatience at what Shaw would do next. "And you're pretty wet yourself." She placed her arms around his neck as the top three buttons of her blouse came undone.

As the last buttons opened, revealing Brandy's lacy bra, she held her breath. Shaw might have felt her nakedness last night, but he had not seen her bare body—no man had. She usually felt so shy, even in front of a camera with little more than a few scraps of material covering her most intimate parts . . . why did she feel so eager for Shaw to see her?

Shaw kissed the side of her neck, his hands massaging the swells of her breasts through the thin barrier of her bra. *How restricting clothes can be,* thought Brandy, winding her arms tighter around his neck, her fingers spreading into his hair.

Shaw's kisses dropped lower, his hand sliding behind her back to unclasp her bra. "Will Eric stay in his room?" he asked as he lifted his head, his eyes smoky with desire as they devoured her flushed face and heaving breasts.

"Oh! Eric! I forgot about him."

"Relax." Shaw grinned at her expression. "At least we're making progress if I can make you forget about Eric for a few minutes."

Brandy couldn't reply to that.

"We'd better adjourn to the bedroom for safety's sake," he whispered, effortlessly scooping her up in his arms to carry her there. "Still sore?" His grin widened at her protests.

"I wasn't faking, you know," she retorted. *At least not completely,* she added to herself.

"I know." He smiled, his voice soft and concerned.

He was at the door of the bedroom when the phone rang. Brandy was tempted to tell him just to ignore it, and as he hesitated with her in his arms, she thought he was probably considering doing just that. Convention got the better of him, though, and he set her gently on her feet. "I won't be long." His smile was a promise of what was to come.

Brandy clung to him for a moment as he steadied her.

"Are you okay on your feet?"

She nodded, her hands reluctant to leave his strong, warm body. "I can manage."

Shaw turned back into the living room and in two long strides reached the phone. Brandy saw him glance back at her lingering in the doorway. What was it about the man that attracted her? she thought. Why had she chosen him for a husband? What was she doing waiting patiently, even eagerly, for him to take her?

She was so lost in her bewildering thoughts that it took several moments before she realized Shaw was speaking to another woman: one of his many girlfriends, no doubt, she thought, and one who obviously expected him to be with her at that moment.

The phone call brought Brandy back to her senses. He was nothing but a playboy. Tonight, she happened to be the object of his attention—probably because she was simply the closest at hand. The fact that they were married made no difference to him. He would take what he wanted when it was offered to him.

But she was not offering any longer, if she could help

herself. As she wondered if she could keep to this decision, she slammed the bedroom door shut and locked it behind her.

Shaw hung up the phone almost immediately after the door slammed and started pounding on it.

"Open this door, Brandy. Right now."

"No." She was halfway across the room now, wondering if he could open it despite the lock. He might have a key somewhere in the apartment for emergencies, but she wondered if he'd know where to find it. No female had probably *ever* locked him out of a bedroom before.

"I'm warning you, Brandy, you'd better open this door."

"Why?" she demanded. "So you can continue using your charms on me? I may be your wife, Shaw Janus, at least for the moment, but that doesn't mean you can treat me like the rest of your casual affairs."

"You didn't seem to be objecting to my treatment a minute ago," he countered.

She was momentarily speechless. "I suppose you think all a model does is stand in front of a camera and pose . . . but I know a lot about acting, too."

Shaw muttered something she couldn't understand.

"What did you say?" she shouted.

"Nothing!"

"Good. If you still have any romantic ideas for the evening, why don't you take them up with your girl-friend? It sounds as if she was expecting you tonight, anyway. I suppose she didn't realize you were occu-pied. And don't expect me to be so cooperative any-more."

There was no reply through the door, which worried

Brandy more than Shaw's taunts. She made a few more nasty comments, and receiving no response, she stomped her way across the room to the bath. A good hot shower was the first thing she needed. Once she calmed down and got out of her wet clothes, she could think about her next move, she thought. She couldn't stay locked in here all night, if only out of decency to Shaw. All of his clothes were in here, and he could be needing a warm bath, also. Of course, he could use Eric's bath, but he would still need fresh clothes.

As Brandy finished the job Shaw had begun of undressing her, she realized she needed clothes worse than Shaw did. She could always place a bundle of his things just outside the door, but she had nothing to wear until he brought her clothes up from the car. In the mood he was in right now, he wouldn't be too excited about doing any favors for her.

Brandy had been lucky enough to escape Shaw that evening, but she realized it would only be a matter of time before his stronger will won their battle.

Finishing her bath, and with a towel wrapped around her hair, she pulled on his long terry robe. She had heard him leave the apartment and hoped it was to collect her clothes. She took the opportunity to bundle together a selection of his clothes, deposit them outside the bedroom door, and locked herself in again, pulling the bedcovers high over her head so she wouldn't hear him if he began pounding on the door again.

After he returned, she heard him turn the knob at the bedroom door, but when the door didn't budge, he retreated. As nervous as she was, Brandy must have fallen asleep quickly, the strain and anxiety of the long

day finally catching up with her, because the next thing
she knew, Shaw's alarm clock, which she had set in
time to get Eric ready for school, was buzzing her
awake.

Brandy sat up in bed, pulling Shaw's robe, which had
served as her nightgown, around her bare body. *Will I
end up back in this bed tonight, with him?* she wondered. She couldn't decide if that frightened her more
than the thought of Shaw in someone else's bed that
night.

She shook her head free of the thoughts. Shaw was
his own man. He would take what he wanted when he
was ready. She had deterred him last night purely for
the moment.

In the bathroom, Brandy splashed cold water on her
face and checked her clothes. They were still damp, and
she was still at Shaw's mercy, confined to his robe.

She was reluctant to parade out into the living room
dressed as she was, even if the garment was totally
concealing. Shaw would know it was the only thing she
had on, and he would probably take advantage of the
fact, but she had to wake Eric and get him ready for
school. Besides, Shaw had thought of Eric last night
during the heat of their lovemaking. If he could do that,
then surely she was safe from his advances—as long as
Eric was around. But what would happen after she
took Eric to school?

She couldn't bear thinking about it, noticing the
seductive curves of her breasts reflected in the mirror,
and wondering how she would look through Shaw's
eyes. Her body was aroused at the mere thought of
him, and that angered her. With his countless affairs,
she didn't approve of what he stood for. *Stop it*, she
told herself, tying the sash of the robe tightly about her

waist. She had to wake Eric now. She'd just have to handle things one at a time.

She found the door unlocked. *So he did know how to get to me. Then why hadn't he?* she wondered.

She left the door wide open as she left the bedroom. Shaw had proved a locked door would never stand between him and the woman he wanted: she suspected very little else would either, when he was ready to make his move.

Eric's door was ajar, and when she peered in she found the covers thrown back and the bed empty. The bath was vacant, too, and as she puzzled about where he might be, she heard him giggle from the direction of the kitchen.

Brandy padded across the deep pile carpet to the kitchen to find Eric swinging his legs from his chair, crumbling toast, and laughing at something Shaw had said to him. Her movement at the door caught his eye and he turned and smiled at her.

"Good morning, sleepyhead," Shaw drawled, his gaze stripping her of the robe and placing her back in bed.

Brandy blushed, surprised to see Eric fully dressed and hair combed, and breakfast all but finished. "It's not that late, is it?"

"Electricity went off during the night," Shaw explained casually, pouring coffee and offering her a cup.

Brandy, who normally didn't drink coffee, was so surprised by his show of domesticity that she accepted, and sat somewhat awkwardly in the chair Shaw pulled out for her at the table beside him. "Black?" he asked.

"What?" She had been taking in the collection of pots Shaw had added to her mess from the evening before. Evidently he was adept at cooking ham and eggs and toast, not to mention the fresh-squeezed orange juice she noticed in the pitcher in front of them. "No, the works."

Shaw slid the cream and sugar containers in front of her and continued to eye her softly curling hair and full lips as she tended to her coffee cup.

He was wearing jeans and a shirt from the pile she had left out for him.

"I see you found your clothes," she said unnecessarily.

"Hmmm," he answered.

"Where did you sleep?"

"On the couch," he replied, asking Eric if he'd like a refill.

Brandy was tempted to ask whose couch—his own or someone else's—but a second look told her she had better not push her luck.

"What time is it?" she asked, leaning forward to read the hands on Shaw's watch.

"Seven-thirty. Just enough time for me to shave and change clothes before dropping Eric off at school. I thought you'd never wake up."

Brandy blinked. He was acting as if they had been through this routine for years. Had this been what she had glimpsed in Shaw? That ability to take charge of a situation?

"That's kind of you, Shaw, but I'll get dressed . . . you did bring my clothes up, didn't you?"

He nodded. "In my closet."

Her mouth dropped open. Not only had he managed to unlock the bedroom door, but had actually entered the room and hung up her clothes while she was sleeping. "I—I'll take Eric to school. I don't want to put you out."

"It's on the way for me, and I have to be at the office about the same time he's supposed to be at school, so it's no trouble."

"Still—"

"It's no problem," he cut into her words. "Besides, Eric and I have a lot to talk about, don't we?" He winked at the small head beside him.

Eric nodded up and down like a co-conspirator, and Brandy wondered what the two of them could have in common after such a brief acquaintance. Still, if they were to be living together for the next few weeks, or months, it was probably best that they get to know each other.

She couldn't help wondering what the topic of their conversation was, and challenged, "Like what?"

"Oh, various things," Shaw said vaguely, "like certain people we both know."

She blushed. Shaw was using Eric, pumping him for information about her. What the poor child could be telling him she could hardly guess, but it rankled nevertheless. She'd just have to have a talk with Eric about it.

"Did you know Shaw has an airplane, Brandy?"

"It's Mr. Janus," she corrected him.

"But he said I could call him Shaw," Eric pouted. "He's not my father, but he's like a big brother. I don't want to call him Mister."

"It's okay, Eric," Shaw intervened. "I want you to call me Shaw. Mr. Janus sounds so old."

Eric beamed. "Shaw has an airplane," he picked up the thread of his conversation as if he had never been interrupted, "and he says he'll take me for a ride in it. Won't that be swell?"

Brandy wasn't so sure, but she smiled and kept her

opinions to herself. At least they weren't discussing her all of the time; they were talking about her enough, though, to make her feel outnumbered.

"Well." Shaw pushed his plate aside, and got up from the table. "I'm going to have to hurry if I don't want to be late. Do you mind washing the dishes?"

Brandy looked at the mound of kitchenware in the sink and shook her head. She felt as if she were watching a movie of someone else's life.

Shaw was at the door when he turned back and cast a lecherous look in her direction. "What do you have planned today?" he asked.

Brandy blinked, grasping for some sense of reality. Her entire life had turned upside down in twenty-four hours. What was she going to do about it? she wondered. "I'm not sure. Regroup and rearrange, I guess. I need to contact my agent and let him know how to get in touch with me."

"We're going to have a long talk about your 'career' one day—soon," he promised before he left the room to dress for work.

Brandy stared dazedly after Shaw, eventually realizing Eric was trying to get her attention with all of his talk about Shaw's airplane. It was a four-seater, so there'd be room enough for her, too, he was telling her. *Just enough extra space,* thought Brandy, *for one of Shaw's girlfriends, to tag along, also.*

She stood up, deciding that it was time to tackle the pile of dishes. Eric was babbling on about the airplane as if he was planning to take it to class for one of his "show and tell" projects. Her attempts to change the subject and probe into Shaw's investigation of her went unheeded. Eric was too wound up, tighter than a propeller, on the subject of airplanes to want to talk about anything else. Brandy grinned. Maybe Shaw would have just as much trouble changing the subject as she. *Serve him right,* she thought.

She had just finished washing the last pot and had begun drying the plates when Shaw poked his head around the kitchen door. "You must be quite good at method acting." He startled her.

"What?" She turned around, smiling at the complimentary tone of his voice.

"You get so involved in your roles," he commented. "Anyone looking at you right now would think you were quite a happy little wife, but we both know better, don't we?"

Brandy fixed a grin on her face, refusing to rise to his taunts in front of Eric. "I do hope you have a nice day, Shaw. I'm sure I will after you leave."

"Well?" He hadn't moved from the door.

"Well what?"

"Aren't you going to kiss me goodbye?" His brief glance at Eric implied: this had better be good, unless you want Eric to get the wrong idea about his happy new home.

"How could I forget?" She rushed over to him, intending to peck him on the cheek, but before she could, Shaw caught her in his arms, bending her almost double so that she was entirely at his mercy as his lips plundered her own.

She was breathless when he left her, half from the position he had thrown her into, and half from the devastating kiss. Her legs felt wobbly, that same fluttery feeling she experienced last night in his arms invading her entire body.

"I'll see you tonight," he whispered, eyes gleaming at her disheveled appearance, "and we'll establish a few ground rules."

"Don't count on it," her eyes replied, but she didn't utter another word until both he and Eric were out of the apartment and far enough away not to hear her scream of frustration. What could she do? Shaw Janus was her husband in name. It was only a matter of time before he became her husband in deed as well.

Chapter Five

After Brandy got dressed she decided the first thing to do was call her agent. As she dialed the number she hoped he would be in and would have some work for her. She was tired of talking to his secretary and being told, "Sorry, but we haven't had calls for a girl with your height." Being two inches short of the high fashion standard was beginning to get her down. It wasn't supposed to be such a hindrance to girls anywhere but in New York City, but she was beginning to feel it was a burden.

Dean Nixon was out the first time she called, and rather than have his secretary deliver a message, which Brandy often wondered if he ever received, she found out when he would be expected back in the office and called later that morning. Although the secretary was reluctant to put her call through to him, Brandy finally heard his voice.

"How ya doin', babe?" he asked, as always.

"Just fine." She always lied. "I was hoping you might have some modeling assignments for me. It's been over a month since—"

"Aw, babe, you know how it is."

No, I don't, she thought. *I'm trying to figure it out.*

"They just don't ask much for girls with your hair color. All the photographers want blondes these days. Did you ever think of dying your hair?" he suggested.

"If it would help, I would. But I just don't see—"

"And it's your height. They like them tall and skinny. Back to the Twiggy look."

"But I keep seeing all these girls with dark hair and . . ." her voice trailed off.

He would have an answer if she said she could change her hair color at will. It was getting discouraging to talk to her agent these days, and that was a shame. It used to excite her so much just to hear all the enthusiasm he had about her future. But that was before she had paid her registration fee. She had later learned— the hard way—that most agents work solely on a commission from the work they get for a model. He had already gotten her all the work he had guaranteed he could get for her, and since that time the assignments had dwindled more each month while his excuses became more inventive.

"Look," she said finally, mustering the courage to tell him exactly what she thought, "I just don't think you're doing the job you're supposed to be doing for me. I'm not like some of these girls who are working two jobs and have to maneuver around their delicate schedules to accept modeling positions. I can go anywhere, anytime. I have my own car. I don't have to wait for taxis or buses. I can do my own makeup and hair and change it enough to look like several different people. Why can't you get me more jobs?" The speech was against her nature, but maybe she was becoming more outspoken—she could thank Shaw for that influence.

"Well, I'll level with you, babe. It's your composite."

A mental image of her representative photographs flashed through her mind. "What's wrong with it?"

"The pictures . . . they're just not up to professional quality," he explained.

She had to admit some of the shots were not too flattering, but she had put together the best photos she could get at the time with the help of the only photographer she could afford.

"If I don't have a good composite to present to a client, they're not going to want to use the girl. Now, if you had another composite made, one a little bit more revealing of your, ahem, character, I might be able to get you more work. Find a good photographer and lay out some money on a top-notch composite. You know what they say—"

"No, I don't," she pouted, remembering the cost that had been involved with that first composite.

"You have to spend money to make money."

She sighed. That was just what she needed to hear right now. Still, she had to agree her composite didn't look as slick as those of some of the girls' that she had met during assignments.

Her agent hemmed and hawed with a few more excuses a while longer. He would not promise anything, but said he would see if he could get her a job or two to help pay the bills if she would just get another composite done.

Brandy sank into the sofa after the phone call. Even if she could get the photos shot tonight, it would be weeks before she could give her agent a new composite. Weeks without work. Now, more than ever, it seemed to her as if Shaw Janus was not only Eric's last hope, but her own as well.

She drove to her apartment a few hours later, and stuffed as many of her belongings as she could manage into her car. Her landlady was out, so she left a note saying she'd try to stop by for tea one afternoon, and that Shaw would help her move the rest of her belongings out of the way that weekend. She didn't doubt that people would be lining up for the charming little efficiency. It was in one of the best neighborhoods and, at least when she was renting, priced way below anything of lesser quality that she had found. As Brandy drove away, she wondered where she would find to live once Shaw divorced her. It didn't do much good worrying about it now, but she couldn't help herself. Since Eric had come to her, she seemed to do nothing but worry.

She even worried about what to fix for Shaw's supper that night. Meat and potatoes, he had said. It sounded dull to her, even if it was a chance to eat real meat rather than cheaper cuts of chicken or fish. She had thrown a few of her favorite cookbooks into the car; perhaps she could find some exotic way to spice up the meat and serve the potatoes with a flair.

She picked up Eric from school and tried to pump him again about what he and Shaw had talked about concerning her, but he was involved with thoughts of an upcoming school outing to an amusement park, and it was all she could do to work in a casual "Hello."

Dinner was simmering in its last stages on the stove when Brandy heard Shaw's key in the lock. She wondered if she should rush to greet him at the door. A loving wife would, but she didn't want him to get the wrong idea.

She stood in the doorway of the kitchen as he came in, and smiled. It wouldn't help any of them to look glum. Besides, she had gone to the trouble of cooking this meal for him.

He wasn't frowning, and she took that for a good sign. But he didn't respond to her smile. "How was your day?" she asked, for lack of a better opening.

"Peachy keen," he answered sarcastically.

She kept her lips fixed in a smile, watching him wearily shed his tie and jacket and drop his briefcase on the bureau. What would it take to perk him up? she wondered, then arrived at the logical suggestion. "Would you like a drink?"

His eyes nailed her to the wall. "I'm beginning to wonder if I should ever accept a drink from a stranger again. You, in particular."

"Oh." She dropped the smile altogether. "Because I got you drunk last time."

The memory did not amuse him.

"How about some lemonade?" she offered hesitantly.

"Scotch will be fine." He sprawled on the couch and kicked off his shoes. "Well?" he goaded as she hovered in the doorway. "What are you waiting for?"

"Where do you keep it?"

"I thought you would have run across it by now. In the kitchen cabinet over the dishwasher, next to the cooking sherry."

Brandy found the cabinet and glasses, filled his with Scotch, and hers and Eric's with lemonade.

"Are you hungry?" she asked Shaw as she handed him his drink.

"You shouldn't have bothered cooking," he returned. "I could have gotten something at the restaurant."

But he hadn't. She asked, "Are you going out later?"

"Maybe." He sniffed the air. "What's for supper?"

"Meat and potatoes."

"Doesn't smell like any kind of meat and potatoes I ever ate."

Brandy sighed. She could tell it would be a real educational process to change his eating habits. Why should she bother? she wondered. It would only be for a few months, but right now it was the only way she could think of to tell him how grateful she was. "The potatoes are au gratin."

"I think I've run across something like that on a menu once or twice. Do you cook like this all the time?"

"When I have time, I like to. But not when it's just for me. It's not too much fun eating alone," she added.

"That it is not." He downed the rest of his Scotch and held out his glass for another.

"Sure?" She didn't want to be accused of taking advantage of him again.

"One more, but I'll take it after I shower."

Brandy held her breath, half expecting him to make some kind of remark about her joining him to scrub his back, but whether he was thinking in terms of Eric's impressions or just too tired to banter with her, he left the living room without a further word.

In the kitchen Brandy finished making salad, then laid the napkins beside the plates. If she couldn't earn her own way with her modeling, at least she could keep Shaw's apartment clean and meals on the table. Maybe he would eventually realize having her around was not going to be such a traumatic experience. Time would tell.

"What would you like for dinner tomorrow night?" Brandy asked Shaw as he lingered over a second cup of coffee after dinner. Their conversation over the meal had been quite civilized, and even Eric had joined in with chatter about his day in school and how all the boys in his class had reacted to the news of Shaw's airplane and his promise to take Eric for a ride.

Eric sat in front of the television set, his lessons finished, eating a bowl of ice cream while Brandy and Shaw shared coffee at the kitchen table.

"I don't know," he said, "I may not be home tomorrow night."

"Can I fix something cold, then, that you could eat at any time after you arrive home?"

"Don't bother."

"It's no bother." She smiled, eager to please him. He had been so nice over dinner, taking such an interest in Eric's school day. She wanted to show him how much she appreciated that. "I could fix some tuna salad or—"

"I said, don't bother."

Brandy paused. She was beginning to see the "Jekyll and Hyde" in his personality, and she could not understand it. "What's the matter, Shaw?" Her eyes revealed her concern, but Shaw interpreted it as a look of pity.

"I'm not sure how much of this domestic scene I can take," he flared. "You don't look the part—washing, scrubbing, cooking, and cleaning."

"I was raised to do my own housekeeping. I don't mind."

"Well I do," he said. "I don't need a housekeeper. I already have one. She comes in whenever I call her. And as far as a cook—I've eaten most of my meals out."

"But you don't have to now. I love to cook." She wanted to add how much she had enjoyed the look of awe mingled with appreciation on his face when he tasted her meal this evening, but he interrupted her.

"Let me put it this way," he grated, speaking slowly so that she would not miss a word he said. "The day I accept you as my housewife, there are going to be a lot of other rights included with that role."

Brandy blushed. The tension was between them again, thick and heavy as pea soup. For Brandy it was a threat, but Shaw didn't know that. "I thought we settled that last night."

"Did we? In what way?"

Brandy started picking up the plates to keep from looking at the way he was seeing her, without clothes, across the living room, in his bed. He reached out, his hand on hers, forcing her to look at him and face his question.

"I, we," she faltered, "I mean, you said you didn't want me restricting your life. Fine. Then I want the same rights. I don't care to sleep with you."

She held her breath, wondering how she was going to

have the nerve to reinforce her feelings with reason. If she told him that he had not actually consummated the marriage the first night, that all that bound them together was a slip of paper, however legally it was signed and filed, then she might as well say goodbye to his aid with Eric's custody case. All that bound him to her was some sense of righteousness he vaguely felt for having slept with her. He felt guilty about that, confused, too, about how it had all happened, but that guilt and confusion were the paste and glue that held him to her in marriage. To admit that he did not owe her a thing would be admitting defeat. And she couldn't do that when he seemed to be accepting the idea.

He wasn't taking her answer very well. "I won't force you." He stared right through her. "I tried that last night and I've never needed to force a woman to love me. However," he smiled, infuriating Brandy with his smug look, "I don't think you'll mind too much. You didn't put up a very convincing fight last night."

"That's only because I hadn't had time to think everything through," she retorted. "But today I have, and I don't feel it's necessary to be bribed into bed with you. Either you want to help me as far as Eric is concerned, or you don't. Your bed is not going to be part of the bargain. I'll sleep with Eric."

Shaw lounged back in his chair absorbing all that she said. "I've already said I won't force you. I don't think I'll have to. You'll come willingly enough."

"Don't hold your breath waiting."

"I won't. But don't be surprised when you find yourself in my bed—for Eric's sake."

Brandy didn't like the way he was smiling at her. As if he knew something she didn't. She wondered if it could have anything to do with the little talk he had with Eric about her this morning. What could Eric have possibly told him?

She picked up the plates with a clatter that nearly broke them. "You may have most women wrapped around your little finger, Shaw Janus, but I'm not in the same class as them. I will not be bribed or blackmailed or badgered into your bed."

"No," he smiled. "Logic is more appealing to you, isn't it?"

"I do think I have a rather practical mind." Somehow that practicality had gotten her involved with this man. She did, at times, have reason to doubt the workings of her own mind.

"I think you'll see how logical it is for you to share my bed."

Brandy didn't answer him.

"It all depends on how important it is for you to keep Eric with you."

"You know that's the most important thing in the world to me."

"I'm counting on it. By the way," he stood, watching her with the dishes, picturing her in an entirely different setting. "I stopped by your apartment."

"Did you? What for?" She turned around, suds dripping from her hands. "I went by today, too."

"I thought I might be able to put a few more things into my car, but your landlady was out and I didn't have the key."

"Oh, dear. I'm sorry you went over there for nothing."

"I did get your mail." He pulled the few letters out of his pocket. She had noticed them during dinner, but thought they belonged to him. "One looks fairly important."

"Which?" she bristled, annoyed that he had, if not read her mail, checked over each piece. Their hands brushed, and lingered in the exchange of envelopes. "Oh," she sank down in the nearest chair. "It's something to do with Eric's custody case."

"Shall I open it for you?" he asked, when she made no move to unseal the letter. Brandy silently handed the envelope back to him, glad that he could take charge. Just the thought of losing Eric upset her and the less she dwelt on the legalities to be faced, the happier she could pretend to be.

"Hmmm," he scanned the contents. "Just a notice to appear in court next week. They don't waste time, do they?"

Brandy sighed. She had known already about the court case. That was why she had been in such a rush to get married. "Will you be able to get away from work to go with me?"

"I guess I'll have to." He stuffed the letter back into the envelope and tossed it onto the kitchen counter. "That's my whole purpose, isn't it?"

Her eyes were big pools of tears. As far as she was concerned, that was exactly how she saw Shaw Janus; but stated in such cold-blooded simplicity, she was beginning to see what an insult that could be to a man, especially one as virile as he. "Thank you," she answered, preferring not to confirm or deny his statement which would so easily lead to an argument.

"I'll try to live up to my end of the bargain," he said, "as I'm sure you will."

"What bargain?" Her head jerked up.

"We don't have one yet," he smiled, "not officially, anyway. But we will, before too long." His voice turned brisk before she could protest or question about his statement. "I think I'll leave you for the evening. I have other, uh, engagements to take care of. Don't bother waiting up."

Brandy could have assured him she wouldn't, but she was still so puzzled, and wary, of his last statement about a pending bargain, that she did not utter a word as Shaw collected his coat and keys and left the apartment.

What bargain does he have in mind? she wondered. *And what price will I have to pay?*

Chapter Six

A few days later, after Shaw left with Eric on the way to work and school, Brandy's agent called. Rich's, one of Atlanta's most exclusive department stores, was having a fashion show that day at noon. One of the runway models had sprained her ankle, and Dean Nixon asked Brandy to substitute. She usually jumped at the chance to do any kind of modeling, and this time she particularly needed the money to have another portfolio and composite made. The show would take place in one of the restaurants at the extensive Peachtree Plaza complex, and her job was to mingle with the diners while showing off her outfits.

She was so excited about the job she nearly sprained

her ankle in the rush to collect her makeup, curlers and undergarments required for the different outfits she would have to model. She had little experience with this type of modeling, but knew she would have to be there as early as possible to memorize details about the dresses and sportswear she would wear. If any of the diners asked her questions, she had to be prepared with the correct answers, which could earn her a reputation as a reliable model.

Brandy seldom had the opportunity to visit the Peachtree complex. She had, in fact, only wandered through the building once out of curiosity and wonder. The wide, open foyers with cascades of geraniums and vines spilling a distance of one and two stories between floors had fascinated her. She had ridden the escalator in order to enjoy the view, but today she was in a hurry, and not quite certain exactly where she was supposed to go to prepare for the luncheon show.

Luck seemed to be with her when she recognized another model hurrying to catch one of the elevators on its way down. She followed the other girl and soon realized the fashion show would be in the lower level restaurant of the complex called Off Peachtree.

Each of the girls was given five outfits to model, which seemed quite a lot to Brandy as she noticed the size of the restaurant and the zigzagging course laid out between the tables. When she read the card accompanying the first outfit her nerves jangled further. How would she ever remember all of this information, especially if every outfit required such detailing? she wondered. Fortunately, as she was handed a terry sports outfit, another dress and two swimsuits, she found only two of the descriptions would make her feel as if she were reciting the Gettysburg Address.

The first dress was layered in voile, and accented with flounces and little ties. Brandy was glad to be getting that one out of the way. She stepped out into the restaurant wending her way around the tables with a stomach full of butterflies, but by the time she reached the last table and gave her speech correctly and informally, her confidence won out over the nerves.

She hurried into the changing room for the next outfit, a day dress in bold colors and wide stripes, worn with a simple white bolero jacket. She was shocked to find the dress a size too big, but the bolero covered her enough in case one of the straps of the dress decided to stray off her shoulder.

Brandy's confidence was reflected in the way she walked and in her lighthearted voice. Several ladies stopped her to ask questions about the dress, which she was relieved she could adequately answer. One man had her spin around an extra time—so he could see the cut of the dress, he said. If she had not been wearing the semi-concealing bolero, she might have doubted his word.

The terry sports set was next, strapless and chic. The selling point of this particular outfit was the well-known designer, so Brandy finished her speech at each table in record time—but the man at the center table, who had expressed such interest in the last outfit, found plenty to say about it. Brandy was beginning to think twice about his interest, especially when he started to ask how easily it came off.

She stalked away as politely as she could, and hurried to change into the next piece: a flowing caftan of rich hues of blue from turquoise to peacock to midnight, all deftly blended one into the other, with underneath, a shocking-pink bikini. *Mr. Inquisitive is going to love this,* she thought, concentrating on her lines and hoping he wouldn't embarrass her.

She avoided looking in his direction as she emerged, taking little courage in the fact that some of the other girls were giggling about his leering looks: at least it proved he wasn't singling her out. If she took longer at the first table, she could hurry at his to try to make up her lost time, and maybe cut short his delaying remarks in the process.

Because she was avoiding the center table, Brandy didn't notice when Shaw Janus walked into the room and joined her admirer at his table. Shaw was just apologizing for being late when Brandy heard and recognized his voice. Her heart beat faster as she caught sight of him.

Brandy came up behind Shaw's companion and smiled shyly. Her sudden appearance nearly caused Shaw to choke on the water he had just put to his lips. "What the—"

Looking straight at Shaw, directing all of her narrative solely for his benefit, she warmed to her subject. She knew she looked good in the outfit, seductive even, and it was safe to look that way for Shaw—certainly safe with a crowded restaurant of people staring on. She wouldn't dare dress this way if they were alone.

"What is going on here?" Shaw managed to finish his sentence.

"It's a fashion show," Shaw's companion answered. "Quite a selection of desserts, don't you think?" He reached out and patted Brandy as if he had arranged the entire show for Shaw's benefit.

Brandy jumped at his familiarity while Shaw muttered through gritted teeth, "Take your hand off of her, Wayne."

Wayne laughed, his hand still in the folds of Brandy's caftan.

"Please," she whispered, not wanting to create a scene, but resenting the man's hand, and embarrassed that Shaw should see her in such a predicament.

"I said," Shaw repeated, "take your hand off of her."

"Shaw," the man removed his hand, a big grin spreading over his face, "where's your sense of humor?"

Shaw glared at him while Brandy took the opportunity to escape to the next table. Her mind was only half on the description of the caftan as she overheard Wayne say, "The way you're acting, a man would think she was your wife."

Brandy paused in her talk, straining to catch Shaw's answer, but she couldn't hear whether he admitted it or not.

One outfit to go, and it was the most revealing—a "swiss cheese-cut" swimsuit that had barely enough "swiss" to cover her "cheese." The coverup wasn't much of one either—a sheer shortie negligee. She wished Shaw had arrived much earlier and gone already, but she knew as she tucked her hair beneath a floppy straw hat that nothing in the world would get him to leave now. At least she wouldn't have to put up with the other man's pawing, though.

A blush had started on her neck and spread to her face before she even advanced to the second table in the restaurant. Shaw's eyes followed her every movement, and try as hard as she might she found it difficult to avoid his eyes as she modeled the swimsuit.

His own face seemed darker than usual. As little time as Brandy had been with him she still recognized the signal as mounting anger. Well, she was very sorry if he and his friend were at odds because of her, she thought. She had not asked Wayne to manhandle her, and she had not acted impolitely in spite of her acute embarrassment. It would be bad for the store's policy if she did anything but remain calm and pleasant despite any treatment the audience handed out. Shaw had no reason to be mad at *her* for his friend's bad taste.

Lifting her head higher, she glided to their table and forced her most dazzling smile upon them. Shaw's frown deepened, but Wayne's eyes glittered more than ever. "I have to admit," Wayne said after Brandy had delivered her brief description of her garments, "you sure can pick 'em, Janus. If he ever gets tired of you, honey, look me up." He winked at Brandy.

Brandy glanced hastily from one to the other. Shaw wasn't saying a word, but she was certain he would save up enough for the first moment they were alone. She couldn't say she was looking forward to that night—not that she would otherwise have been eagerly awaiting Shaw's arrival.

"How many more of these outfits are you going to . . . display?" Shaw caught her wrist as she was about to leave their table.

"This is the last one," she said, her voice barely above a whisper. She swallowed. "Let go of me, Shaw. It'll throw everyone out of sequence."

"When will you be finished?" he demanded, his thumb massaging the inner softness of her wrist. It only served to make her more aware of him, and more aware of how much of her body he was seeing.

"Whenever all of the other girls finish."

"I'll take you home."

"I have my car." The last thing she wanted was to be

alone with him in a confined compartment. "But thank you." It wouldn't hurt to try to appease him with a little politeness.

Wayne interrupted whatever Shaw had intended to say by commenting, "First argument, you two?"

"It's none of your business," Shaw snapped. Brandy was relieved that someone else was getting the benefit of his temper.

She slipped her wrist out of his grasp and continued to the next table, so upset she didn't even realize she was describing the last swimsuit she had worn until the woman glanced up at her and said, "Oh, does this come in shocking pink, also?"

Brandy smiled and edged away, leaving the woman's question hanging in the air. She was still shaking thirty minutes later when the last girl came out of the restaurant and Rich's fashion coordinator began expressing his delight at the success of the show. Brandy was relieved that no one had noticed the exchange at Shaw's table.

She finished dressing, brushed out her hair and packed up her belongings. "Young lady," the fashion coordinator sidled up to her.

Oh dear, thought Brandy, *he did notice!*

"Yes, sir?" her lower lip trembled.

"I noticed you made quite an impression on several of the gentlemen in the audience," he commented.

"Yes, well, I can explain, sir," Brandy replied haltingly.

"You don't have to explain, my dear. It's quite obvious. You're a beautiful girl. Men are attracted to you. It makes for good business in the fashion world."

Her lower lip dropped. "Then you're not upset?"

"Lord no!" He laughed. "Tantalize and tease. Always keep them guessing. It confuses them so much they think it's the clothes and we have them rushing in the store to buy the same thing for their wives and girlfriends."

"Oh," she said, not knowing if that was how the business really worked or if this were merely his opinion. "I hope that I've contributed to the success of the show."

"You have, my dear, you have." He looked her up and down, then asked, "Dean's agency sent you over, didn't they?"

"Yes, that's right."

"Then they should have your name and address on file."

"Yes, I mean, no. I just moved and my agent only has my phone number. Here—" She dug through her purse for a slip of paper. "I'll write it down for you. My schedule is very flexible and I enjoyed today so much. I hope I can be of service to the store again."

"I'm certain we can work something out." He smiled, and Brandy missed the leer in his eyes as she scrawled her particulars on the piece of paper.

"Thank you, sir." She held out her hand. "It's been a pleasure working with you today."

"The pleasure was entirely mine," he assured her. "Shall I walk out with you?"

"Yes, of course." She glanced around, surprised to see that nearly everyone else had already gone. She picked up her purse and compact suitcase.

The fashion coordinator put his arm around her shoulder. Brandy didn't know how to inform him she would prefer he not be so familiar, so she kept both hands on her bags and her body as stiff as possible.

"We're planning another show in a few weeks," he revealed.

"It must keep you very busy arranging these productions," she answered, trying to keep the talk strictly business.

"Very busy," he commiserated, "and it's difficult keeping a bevy of girls in mind who have the right figure for the type of clothes we're trying to sell."

Brandy nodded, hoping he would ask her to be in the next show, but not wanting to seem too pushy by asking outright.

"I was watching you today." His eyes swept over her again. She pretended not to notice. "I was impressed. Very youthful, yet mature, very . . ." he gestured with his right hand as if it would help him find the word he sought, "full-bodied."

"Thank you," she said as they went out the door. "I know I'm a little short."

"I don't think anyone noticed today when you were wearing that last swimsuit."

"Where will your next show be?" She tried to steer him back to the original subject of the conversation.

"Around the pool of the Hyatt Regency."

She nodded.

"I wonder—"

"Yes?" She held her breath.

"I wonder if you'd like to try out a few other suits for me at my office—say one day next week? Depending on how things work out, I might be able to fit you into the show. I like to work with girls with whom I have a good—personal rapport. You understand, I think?" He smiled at her.

"Oh, of course," she assured him, her mind latching

onto the possibility of earning more money and gaining experience. "When should I come by?"

He dug in his pocket for his card. "Noon, I think. There should be less interruptions then. Shall we say Tuesday?"

"I'd be delighted." She smiled, pleased that she had made an impression on the man in such a short time. As she looked at him, she noticed Shaw glowering at her from the side of a nearby potted palm and knew he had heard most, if not all, of their conversation. By the expression on his face, which she had to admit had not altered from the way he had looked when she had left the restaurant thirty minutes earlier, he was not pleased. "But I'm not certain if I'll be free then." She disentangled herself from his side. "May I call you?"

"I don't ask twice," he stated, sizing up Shaw and dismissing him in one glance.

"Oh, well, I—"

"I'm afraid my wife will be unable to keep any sort of appointment with you, next week or any week," Shaw cut in.

"Shaw," Brandy wailed, thinking of the money she needed, "this is my business."

"No," he corrected, grasping her wrist and pulling her out of the fashion coordinator's path, "this is my business now. By your choice, I might remind you."

Brandy glanced from one man to the other, wondering which of them it would be more costly to anger. A second look at Shaw told her she had no choice at all.

"But I'm a model," she argued, knowing it was a losing battle. "I need the—experience."

"*That* kind of experience you can get at home." His eyes narrowed as he sized up the other man.

"Shaw! What are you implying?"

"He knows what I'm implying." Shaw's eyes never left the other man's face.

Brandy shook her hand free of Shaw's and turned to the fashion coordinator. "I'm terribly sorry. I hope you don't think I agree with him," she apologized.

"I *do* have better things to do than stand here and be insulted." The coordinator drew himself up to his full height, which was still somewhat short of Shaw's.

"I really am terribly sorry." Brandy knew it was hopeless to appease him at this stage. "Shaw, apologize."

Shaw just continued to glare at the man, who made a parting comment about jealous husbands and stalked away.

"How could you?" Brandy flew at Shaw. "You've ruined everything!"

"That's your opinion. God, you're naive! Can't you see what the man was after?"

"You're making that up just because I find him more appealing than you. Besides, I would only have gone there for business. My mind doesn't work the way yours does, Shaw."

"I'm well aware of that. Nor does it work the way his does. You're not very experienced in sizing people up."

"No," she pouted. "You're right there. I wouldn't have involved myself with *you* if I'd been better able to judge character."

Brandy saw that her words hit their mark and she immediately regretted saying them, though she couldn't retract them.

"If that's the way you feel, then I don't care if your reputation goes to hell, which it would have done in short order with that jerk!"

"I, you—" Brandy took a deep breath. "I'm sorry. I

guess you meant well. It's just that I need the work so badly."

"Why? You're not exactly living penniless right now, you know."

Tears welled in her eyes. What would her life be like when she and Shaw parted and she didn't have any money saved? "I've already taken too much from you, Shaw, by snaring you into marriage. I can't take your money as well."

"I have enough not to notice."

"It's the idea of the thing. I've never been a leech."

"I don't believe you ever could." His voice softened.

The new tone of his voice and look in his eyes disarmed her, sending delicious shivers down her spine. "I've already taken too much from you," she whispered. "I'm very grateful."

He stared at her for a long moment. "Sometimes it's more blessed to give than to take."

Brandy couldn't look at him. She knew what he meant: he wanted her. It was clearly written in his eyes. But she couldn't give herself to him—not if she wanted an annulment after she gained custody of Eric. Yet, she owed him something.

"I can't, Shaw," she whimpered.

"Why not?" he asked, calmly, not prodding her any longer.

"I wish I loved you." Tears glistened in her eyes.

He raised his hands in exasperation. "God forbid that you ever do. It would only complicate things."

"But don't you see? If I loved you, I could give you everything of myself—but I can't justify that without love."

"This is a useless conversation," he snapped. "Where's your car?" He led her toward the elevator.

"Talking, I'm beginning to see, is never going to get us anywhere."

"I disagree with that. It may not get us where you want us to go, but open discussions can be very helpful," she replied logically.

"Hmmm," he grunted, and Brandy was certain she had not heard the last of his opinions on their relationship.

Chapter Seven

The days between the fashion show and the first court appearance passed with an uneasy and unspoken truce between Shaw and Brandy. Even in such a short span of time, Shaw seemed to have fallen in love with Eric. At times, he was even nice to Brandy, acting almost like a big brother. She wanted to believe Shaw might be accepting her for herself now that he had a better opportunity to know her, but she tried not to raise her hopes. He, like her, was probably just acting so pleasant, protective and "brotherly" for Eric's sake, but he had more reason than ever to be frustrated with her.

Each night she went to bed conscious of tension in the air. Each night she locked the bedroom door knowing Shaw could open it as easily as a matchbook—if he wanted to. But he never did, and that worried her.

Perhaps it was reverse psychology, she told herself, but each night she found herself thinking more and more about what it would be like if he came to her and rightfully shared his bed with her. She even had dreams about it, dreams so warm and sensual she would wake up in the dark and want to run to Shaw asleep on the couch—just to feel his arms around her. She wanted to know that he cared, but she would end up crying herself back to sleep because she knew he didn't. No man did . . . and it would be a long time before anyone could.

Throughout the lonely nights Brandy came to realize something about Shaw's personality. He wanted her, but his pride wouldn't allow him to come to her. No woman had ever turned him down before. He was determined to wait it out with her, tantalizing her with seductive inferences until she would give in to his subtle urgings.

He sent her flowers for no reason. He helped her wash dishes, which secretly endeared him to her because he was filling her fantasy of the kind of perfect domesticity she had always dreamed of one day sharing with a man. And, as he promised, he took Eric and Brandy flying in his airplane, treating Eric with all the respect, awe and delight a real father might show his son.

Brandy wanted to thank Shaw on several occasions for his treatment of Eric. Especially the night before the scheduled court appearance when Eric, sensing the importance of the morning's proceedings, shyly asked Brandy, "Do you think Shaw likes us, Brandy?"

Brandy had been helping Eric get ready for bed. She pulled his undershirt over his head and smiled at him. "I think he likes *you* very much."

Eric's face remained serious as he paused before pulling on his pajama top. "He's been very nice to me." His smooth young forehead puckered into a frown. "Taking me up in his airplane, and letting me go with him to his restaurant and help the chef with all the dinners." His big eyes were round with the importance of the occasion.

Brandy wanted to laugh at his expression, knowing how Shaw had made him feel by introducing him to the restaurant's burly male chef. Even she had been impressed by the astonishing array of pots and pans and the incredible amount of food which could be served and consumed in a single evening.

"Do you think Shaw likes us enough to keep us?" Eric's lower lip quivered.

Brandy scooped him into her arms, unwilling to let him see her eyes. "Of course he does, darling." She sank her teeth into her lip and closed her eyes. At least he did for now, long enough to help her gain custody of Eric. He had even contacted his own attorney about the case, and the attorney had assured Shaw they had every possibility of winning custody.

But how long would he be willing to keep them after that? *Not long,* she told herself. That was all she had asked of him, anyway. She could tell it wouldn't be easy on Eric, having first lost his parents, and then losing Shaw just as he was beginning to fill the void in his life where a father had been. Eric was growing attached to Shaw; so was she, she admitted. But how much of Shaw's attentions were genuine? How much of his actions simply came out of respect for the role he accepted when he agreed to stay married to Brandy?

Some of Brandy's doubts must have seeped through to Eric, because instead of simply accepting her word and bounding off onto another topic, he tightened his grip on her neck and whispered, "I hope he likes us, Brandy, because I like him."

It was at that moment, as Brandy fought against tears, that Shaw poked his head into Eric's bedroom. "What's this?" He grinned a devilish smile that suddenly made Brandy's heart melt. "Aren't you in bed yet?" He advanced into the room as Brandy and Eric drew apart. "I thought I had a date with somebody in here to finish that story about King Arthur and the Knights of the Round Table?"

Brandy sniffed, hoping Shaw would think she had just caught a cold. "Hurry up, Eric." She held out his pajama bottoms for him to step into. "You want to hear how the story ends, don't you?"

"Yes, please, Shaw." He looked up, the smile bigger than ever on his face as his eyes filled with hero worship for the man who sat down on the edge of the bed, close enough for Brandy to feel the heat of his body and, if she leaned back, be able to rub her back against his legs.

"Hurry up, then, Eric," Brandy urged. "Shaw doesn't have all night. He has to get back to the restaurant."

"Not tonight." He lounged back on the bed.

Brandy glanced over her shoulder at him, a quiver of excitement running through her at his smoldering green eyes watching her reactions. "No?"

"No." His eyes left Brandy as Eric bounded onto the

bed next to Shaw and found the place where they had finished reading the previous time.

Brandy hid her surprise. Usually he spent the evenings at the apartment until Eric was asleep, then returned to the restaurant until late into the night. Of course, it was plausible that he could be closing down the place, staying until the last important members of his clientele left; and then he could be working on the accounts until one or two in the morning. She suspected he was spending his nights elsewhere, although once when she had needed to ask where he kept his aspirin when Eric woke up complaining of a sore throat, she had phoned the restaurant and found him there. She decided it was safer not to question why he had decided to stay home that night. He might tell her—or more to the point—he might show her.

"Well." Brandy got up off her knees and began collecting Eric's discarded play clothes. "I'll leave you two gentlemen alone."

"Don't." Shaw reached out and snared her wrist. A fire raced through her entire body from the mere touch of his hand. "Come listen to the story with us."

"Please, Brandy, don't leave," Eric pleaded, sliding down between the blankets as Shaw leaned against the headboard.

Brandy looked from Eric's eager eyes to Shaw's inviting ones, and felt his thumb gently massaging her wrist. Of course she wanted to stay, but should she? She would be safe enough as long as they had Eric between them, she thought.

Shaw had Eric scoot over, and he pulled Brandy onto the bed next to him so that he cuddled Eric against one shoulder, and held Brandy on his other side.

"I'll turn the pages," Brandy offered, hoping she

could do so without giving away how much she bubbled inside.

It took Eric some time to fall asleep that night, and the story was a long one. But Brandy was glad because by the time she had turned to the last page, Eric was sound asleep against Shaw's chest, and she was thinking how nice it was having him hold her close for so long. It would be so easy to love him just because he was so wonderful with children, but she steeled her heart against him. If she let herself fall under his spell, she might not ever want to leave him. She had to do that once she had custody of Eric—this time for Shaw's sake. She had invaded his life. She had no right here despite the legalities. The fact was he did not really want her here. He was merely tolerating her presence until she could win Eric. She would do everyone a favor if she remained uninvolved for the length of her stay. He had already told her he didn't want her to fall in love with him.

Shaw droned the story to an end and Brandy quietly closed the book, but didn't move from his arms. It felt too nice, and she didn't want to disturb Eric. "I can't thank you enough for taking so much time with Eric," Brandy whispered.

"I don't do anything I don't want to do." Shaw let the book fall onto his lap and began rubbing her upper arm. "So don't thank me."

"He's very worried about the court case," Brandy confided, trying to ignore the nervous feeling inside.

"He shouldn't be, nor should you," he yawned. "Wilgus says we have every chance of keeping him."

Brandy noted his use of the word "we" instead of "you." She warmed to his generosity.

"No matter what happens tomorrow," said Brandy,

"I want you to know I'm very grateful after all I've done to you. I can't—" she swallowed back her tears and tried again, "I can't find the words to express just how much it means to me—to us."

He turned his face against her hair, nuzzling against her neck. "Sometimes words aren't adequate in situations like this."

"I know," said Brandy, her heart pounding at his implications. She realized if she had any sense, she would get up off the bed immediately, but if she did, the thought of what would happen next frightened her. It was safer here, with Eric asleep against Shaw's shoulder. He couldn't do much with Eric in the same bed.

Or so she thought.

His hand slipped down her back, snaking between her arm and body to cup her breast, as his lips began an invasion of her senses, tickling and probing her ear and neck and jaw, skipping down to her collarbone and across her shoulder.

"Shaw!" she whispered, trying to stop him, but not wanting to, as his mouth silenced her protests and her body slipped weakly into his arms.

Somehow he managed to settle Eric quietly against the pillow as he slid down on the bed, taking Brandy with him, stretching the length of her so that she could not move for being aware of his hard male body.

"Shaw," she mumbled against his lips, her hands now clinging of their own volition around his neck as her mind struggled for decorum while her body protested against it. "We'll wake Eric. What will he think?"

"Hmmm," he moved his chest from side to side, like a cobra, getting the feel of her breasts tightly against him, "probably that we're very loving parents."

Brandy tilted back her neck so that he could reach it more easily with his tender lips. If only that were true. If only she did love Shaw . . . Her mind protested. That wasn't the problem. If only Shaw loved her . . .

She struggled against him while she still had a shred of sanity, before it was too late. She couldn't let him do this—for his sake—because if she gave in to her feelings for him, she would fight to *keep* him even harder than she had fought to marry him in the first place. That wouldn't be fair to Shaw. He didn't love her. He loved his freedom more. He probably always would. She had bound him to her for the sake of the child. She would not now try to bind him to her for the sake of a one-sided love.

"No!" She shoved against him, and managed to scramble off the bed. "You don't know what you're doing!"

"I know perfectly well what I'm doing!" he hissed, his eyes blazing with unfulfilled desire.

"You don't love me! You just want me!"

"You bet I want you!" He sat up, sliding his legs off the bed, ready to take up where he left off.

"But it's all for the wrong reasons," she argued. "Just because I'm nearby and I'm a challenge to get into your bed, not because you have any decent feelings for me. Your male pride has been wounded because I haven't swooned at your feet—at least not to the degree women usually do in your presence," she qualified, realizing she had to take some of the blame for leading him this far.

"Come here to me," he demanded.

"No!" She stepped back, her eyes darting to Eric stirring beside Shaw in the bed. She lowered her voice. "You don't own me, Shaw Janus."

"Have you forgotten you're my wife?"

"In name only."

His brows rose at that, his throaty laugh an indication that he was remembering how he had woken up with her the morning after their wedding, even if he could not recall the night of the event. "I seem to recall you married me—for the sake of the child."

"And I told you before, Shaw Janus, that was *all* I wanted from you—not the privilege of sharing your bed. If you think you can blackmail me into it, think again. I told you before I will not submit to you, even for Eric's sake. If you don't want to help us, then tell me right now," she stomped her foot for emphasis, "rather than embarrass us in court tomorrow. I don't sleep with anybody in exchange for favors."

A slight blush crept up his neck, as Brandy realized that was precisely what he had intended by staying home that night. Panic raced through her body, replacing all those tenuous feelings of loving and caring she had felt moments before. Was he so callous that he could try to use Eric's welfare to have his own way? Wasn't she guilty of using Shaw for the sake of Eric?

"Well?" she prodded, nauseous with the uncertainty of his intentions. "Are you going to help us or not?"

Eric stirred again beside Shaw, and he turned to look down at the sleeping boy. "You know I'm going to help him."

She had been so tense about his answer, she almost crumpled into a heap at his words. "No," she sighed. "I didn't know."

"But don't think," he stood up, facing her like a duelist who had met his match, "that you'll be sleeping in *my* bed without *me* much longer."

Brandy didn't answer his challenging look. It was

enough for now to know that he was on Eric's side. She could trust him to fight Eric's battle, she would have to fight her own. Without another word, he stalked out of the room and out of the apartment.

The court proceedings went smoothly the next morning, easier than Brandy ever dreamed possible. Shaw's attorney, Max Wilgus, had done his research and was able to fight down every point Louis and May Logan made. Outwardly, Brandy's aunt and uncle could be saccharin-sweet, but Brandy knew they were seething. They had expected to meet Brandy, alone, in court. Instead, they found themselves confronted with the austere scowl of Shaw Janus who acted protective and proprietary toward Brandy and Eric. Anyone seeing them together that morning would have thought they were a couple in love, concerned with a child's welfare, hoping to adopt him into their secure nest. Even more formidable than Shaw was his attorney—one of the top lawyers in Atlanta.

Brandy held her breath when the judge asked how long they had been married, and Shaw answered quite lovingly, "Less than two weeks, sir. The situation did precipitate our feelings for each other, but I have to admit I'm quite glad it did. My wife is rather strong-willed, Your Honor, and it might otherwise have taken me months to convince her to marry me." Brandy kept her eyes on the judge, not daring to look at Shaw. How could he say something like that under oath?

Shaw's attorney went into a lengthy discourse about his client's background and honorability. Brandy said a silent prayer that her sudden appearance with a husband had given her aunt and uncle no time to investigate Shaw's reputation. She couldn't believe it when

the judge finally announced he was giving them custody
of Eric—at least for a trial period in which a welfare
worker would be checking to see how Eric settled into
this new environment.

Brandy was both happy and sad. It would be some
time before they would know for certain if they could
keep Eric. She would have to stay with Shaw for a while
longer. But how much longer after that could she keep
Shaw with her before she would have to give him back
his freedom?

As they were leaving the courtroom a reporter
recognized Shaw, and before he could do anything to
protect Brandy and Eric from the man, they were being
photographed. Shaw muttered under his breath, hustling his family out of the building, "We don't need any
publicity. If that picture gets in the paper with the
slightest reference to my previous reputation, I swear,
I'll sue the paper!"

"Can they do that?" Brandy asked innocently.

"Depends on who that reporter works for. If it's the
Atlanta Constitution, we're probably safe . . . but if it's
one of those underground gossip sheets, we might have
problems."

"Oh, no," Brandy wailed. Her face filled with fear.

"You asked for it, you know." He glared at her, no
longer the image of the loving husband, as he hurried
her into the car with Eric behind him. "Picking me for
husband material. I'm going to have a word with
Wilgus to see if he can suppress this." He slammed the
door shut. "I won't be long."

Brandy bit at her nails while he was gone. He was
right, of course. She should have picked someone more
stable, like Wilgus, for a husband. *Why did I choose
him?* she wondered. It was more than the compassion

she had glimpsed in him: she had to admit that now. He had many fine qualities she could find to love. She had chosen him because she couldn't consider any other man. She had been attracted to him like a moth to a flame from the first moment she had set eyes on him. She had plowed through all the conventions, trapping him in marriage, because her instincts had told her he would help her—and he had. He was going out of his way to help her and Eric. He was a wall of strength against everything that had frightened her such a short time ago. After his actions today, she was finding it more and more difficult to keep from loving him.

I won't think about that, she told herself, looking down at Eric, who was beaming. He understood enough to know he didn't have to go home with Uncle Louis and Aunt May, at least not for a while, and that was enough for him. He did not have to worry ahead to the future the way Brandy did.

Shaw returned and slid behind the wheel. His nut-brown hair was plastered to his forehead from the sweat that had gathered there.

"What did he say?" Brandy asked, wondering if Wilgus could work magic.

"He'll take care of it," Shaw assured her.

Brandy sighed, accepting his word as simply as Eric would have done, and relaxed back in the seat for the drive home.

Shaw pulled up in front of the apartment building, explaining he had work to catch up on and would probably be late coming in. Brandy slid out of the car as Eric skipped into the lobby of the building.

"Hey!" Shaw shouted, as Brandy turned to follow Eric.

She stopped and walked back to the car window, leaning down to hear what he had to say.

"Come around to my side," he said, and Brandy did as he asked. "Don't I get a goodbye kiss? Sort of a thank-you for today?"

Brandy hesitated, the mere thought of touching him filling her with delight and a dangerous awareness of her own increasing susceptibility to him.

"I might as well start working on my new image." He grinned. "Don't you think?"

Brandy smiled, wishing she could impulsively throw her arms around his neck and kiss the daylights out of him.

"Come on." His raised eyebrows invited her closer. "I can't do anything in broad daylight in a parking lot with you outside of the car and me inside of it. And think what good publicity it'll be if someone comes along."

He was right, Brandy decided, and he certainly deserved something. She had to admit that she wanted to kiss him. She bent down, her hands on the door intending to give him a peck on the cheek, but as soon as her head came near his he reached out and caught her neck, imprisoning her lips against his own.

He took his time kissing her, drugging her with the taste of him, teasing her into a response that had her catching her breath and clutching the door to keep from fainting from the weak feeling invading her body.

He finally drew back and looked at her. Why did they have to be here in the parking lot? she wondered. He could make her want him so easily. "Shaw?" she hesitated.

"What?" His eyes smoldered as they looked at her, pleased with what they saw.

Should she tell him what she was thinking? she wondered. Should she try to hide her feelings from him any longer? His eyes continued to hypnotize her. She opened her mouth and whispered, "Try not to be too late tonight?"

His hand slid from behind her neck to caress her cheek. If she wanted to believe in fairy tales, she could say he was actually looking at her with love at that moment. It's only because that's what I want to see, she reminded herself. He smiled, and his eyebrows rose. "I won't be long."

She stood in the middle of the driveway looking after him until the car was gone from sight. Was he acting? Or had she actually glimpsed some concern for her in his eyes? Or was she simply clutching at straws because she wanted him to love her? It would be so simple if he did, because she knew now she could give her heart to him, if he wanted it. If he loved her, and she fell in love with him, then Eric would not have to be uprooted again. But could it be she loved him—*just* for Eric's sake?

Chapter Eight

Brandy remained in a daze after Shaw's sultry kiss. As she and Eric rode the elevator to Shaw's penthouse apartment, she was oblivious to the boy's monologue. Opening the door, she stepped into the living room with her fingers over her lips, still conscious of the feel of his mouth on hers. Was she falling in love with him? Or was she just simply attracted to him physically?

She wandered over to the wide picture window looking out into the distance at downtown Atlanta, the towering silo of Peachtree Plaza and the hazy shapes of the Omni Complex easily recognizable. Where was Shaw at that moment? she wondered. What street would he be driving on? What effect had she had on him? Was he still remembering the kiss, or had he forgotten her the moment he had put the car in gear and driven away?

Because she had him so heavily in her mind, she thought she heard his voice say, "Well, hello." Brandy turned, still in a dream, and stopped at the sight of a man standing in the doorway of the kitchen. Eric, who had plopped down on the couch when they had come into the apartment, stared with widened eyes.

Brandy tried not to panic. She didn't want to alarm Eric. "Who are you?" She took a step toward Eric, mentally looking around the room to remember what would be the nearest thing she could use as a weapon. That lewd brass bust that Shaw kept on the bookcase would be perfect, not only because of its weight, but also because she'd enjoy breaking it.

"I might ask the same of you," said the man, leaning casually against the kitchen doorframe as if he owned the place.

"How did you get in?" She stepped back toward the bookcase.

"With a key, same as you." He smiled.

Brandy's entire body was tense, but she tried not to let it show in her voice. He didn't look like a burglar. In fact, there was something vaguely familiar about him. But that was no reason to trust him. He had no right to be here. "Yes, but this is where I live. I have a right to have a key."

"So have I." The smile widened.

Brandy took another step toward the bookcase. Two more feet and she could reach out and grab the bust—but could she turn and hurl it quickly enough to do any good with him so far away across the room? "Have we met?" she asked cautiously.

"I would have remembered." He pushed himself off

the doorpost and stepped into the room. "Shaw never mentioned you to me either, so this is quite a surprise . . . in a way."

"Shaw?" Brandy breathed a little easier. He had a key and he knew Shaw, but a burglar could have just as much information as access. She wouldn't ease her guard completely. "My husband never mentioned you to me."

"Husband?" He stopped short. Then he laughed. "Shaw? Your husband?"

"Yes. What's so funny?"

He laughed a moment longer, then stopped, his eyes from Brandy to Eric. "Oh, I get it. Husband—for appearances sake."

"No," fumed Brandy. "Husband for legality's sake. Just who are you?"

"I still can't take this in." He started walking across the room. Brandy took that last step backward. "Shaw is the last person I would have expected to find married."

"Nevertheless, it's true."

He laughed. "I have to admire his taste, but then he always did have the cream of the crop at his feet." He scratched his head. "But this is kind of sudden, isn't it? He never breathed a word to me. So you two must still be on your honeymoon. Hmmm." A frown creased his forehead. "I wonder why he invited me here now?"

"Who are you?" Brandy asked again as he kept walking toward her.

"Well," he stopped, folding his arms across his chest, "I guess you could say I'm your brother-in-law. I'm Marcus Janus." He took the last few steps toward her, and held out his hand.

Brandy clutched it, relief making her knees weak. That was why he looked so familiar. It was the shape of his forehead and those eyes. They held the same sensitivity as Shaw's but were gray instead of green. "I thought you were a burglar." She laughed, nerves making her sound giddy. "Shaw didn't tell me you were coming."

"That makes two of us, then, who are surprised. How long have you been married?"

"Not long," she admitted, and as she glanced at Eric, introduced the boy, explaining briefly who he was.

"An instant family," said Marcus, echoing words that Shaw had said to her in anger not long ago. "I can't believe this. Have you known him long?"

"Less than a month," Brandy admitted, blushing at the admiration in his eyes. He was such a contrast to Shaw, tame compared to his brother's almost unruly manner, the kind of man she could feel comfortable around, the kind of man she should have married instead of Shaw. "Oh, excuse me," said Brandy, realizing she had been staring at him and letting her mind wander. "I'm forgetting my manners. Can I get you anything? Coffee? Or something to eat perhaps?"

He laughed, a nice chuckle that was innocent where Shaw's would have been suggestive. "Thanks, but I've already made myself at home. I hope you don't mind, but as I said, I wasn't expecting the likes of you."

"That's perfectly all right." Brandy smiled. "I'm sure Shaw would have wanted you to feel comfortable. I'm sorry he's not here, but he should only be gone a few hours. Will you be staying long?"

"I don't know." He shrugged. "Shaw just wanted me to come. I have no idea why."

"Oh—oh, then you'll be staying the night? Or—"

He grinned again. "I suppose so until I find out what he wants. Who knows? Maybe longer."

"Oh," said Brandy, trying to figure out where everyone, mainly Shaw, would be sleeping while they had company. "Of course you must stay as long as you like." Suddenly she was nervous again, realizing that her tenuous thoughts of inviting Shaw to bed were becoming more of a reality, and in spite of her feelings a few moments ago as Shaw had driven off, she was not certain if she was ready to face the reality.

She looked up at Marcus Janus and wondered if he would understand. She could tell him the truth about how she married Shaw, for Eric's sake, and how Shaw had been sleeping on the couch and she in the bedroom. But should she? They had won the first battle in court today. They needed to do everything they could to reinforce their position as a family. Could she risk telling anyone the truth—even someone as close as Shaw's family? Or should she continue to pretend that they were a loving couple—the perfect parents for Eric.

One thing she knew for certain, Louis and May would go to any lengths to find a chink in the armor—and they wouldn't stop short of using Shaw's relatives if they could. Brandy barely knew Shaw, and she knew nothing about his brother, although she wanted to think he was trustworthy. Still, to play it safe, she decided to pretend to be the loving wife.

"I think I'll fix some coffee." Brandy stepped past him to go into the kitchen. "Then we can get to know each other a little better before Shaw arrives home."

He grinned, a smile that on Shaw would have been a leer, but on Marcus was simply friendly. "There's nothing better I'd like to do than get to know my sister-in-law better."

Brandy learned a lot about Marcus Janus that afternoon as they waited for Shaw to return. He was in some ways very much like his brother; in other ways, they were poles apart. Marcus was younger, just three years older than Brandy. Because of the great difference in his and Shaw's age, Marcus had practically been raised as an only child. Many of the things Brandy told him about her upbringing were familiar to Marcus, also.

She told him all about Eric, and of how she and Shaw were trying to gain permanent custody of him, but she didn't go into detail of how she had tricked Shaw into marrying her. As far as Marcus knew, it truly had been love at first sight for both of them.

Brandy told him all about her hopes and plans to become a top model someday, but confided the difficulty she was having getting jobs. When he seemed disbelieving, she explained that most models were much taller than she, and that she also needed a new composite, but didn't have the money to hire a good photographer. She tried to explain how she wanted to be independent and not make Shaw pay for her expenses, particularly since he did not approve of her career. Then, astonishingly, Marcus offered to loan her the money she needed.

"Oh, but I couldn't take *your* money," said Brandy, awed by his gesture when she had only just met him. "Not any more than I can ask Shaw for it."

"Why not?" He grinned, and Brandy knew he could be almost as persuasive as his brother. "It's all in the family. Besides, I see it as an investment more than anything . . . sort of like owning stock in a racehorse or something. I expect it'll pay off in the long run."

Brandy laughed at being compared to a racehorse, and asked if he thought she remotely resembled a nag. In minutes they were both laughing so hard neither one heard the front door open and Shaw walk into the kitchen where they sat over now-cold cups of coffee.

"Is this a private party, or can anyone join in?" He scowled, and Brandy wondered what had happened at the restaurant to make him so ill-tempered.

"Oh, Shaw!" She scrambled up as quickly as if she had been caught in bed with Marcus—and from the way Shaw's eyes flashed at the two of them, she might as well have been. "I didn't hear you come in."

"Obviously."

"Hello, old man," said Marcus, standing up and extending his hand in greeting. "I must say you don't look too happy to see me."

Shaw's glare was answer enough, but he shook his brother's hand nevertheless.

Brandy looked from one man to the other, the resemblance more obvious now that they stood in the same room. Shaw's attitude confused her. From what Marcus had said, Shaw had summoned him, yet Shaw did not seem too pleased to see him.

"Why don't the two of you get reacquainted in the living room," she suggested, "while I get something started for dinner."

"Don't bother about us," said Shaw, without even looking at Brandy. "We're going out. And it might be late before we get back in. Just make up the couch, will you? For Marcus to sleep on."

So that *was* it. Whether or not Marcus had legitimate business here with Shaw, one service he would be providing was occupancy of the couch—where Shaw had been forced to sleep these past two weeks. That meant, unless she moved in with Eric—which Shaw would probably forbid her to do now that they had a witness within hearing distance of any arguments they might have—Shaw would be sharing his bed with her tonight and every night Marcus remained here.

"But, Shaw—" she protested, feeling trapped, although earlier she had been willing to invite him to bed. She had misread his motives if he would invite his brother there just to give him an excuse to have access to her. Love had never entered his mind. How could it when lust was eating up his heart? she thought.

He stared down at her, his green eyes flashing as if to challenge her to defy him. "I'll talk to you later," he said quietly, but the authority in his voice nailed her to the wall. Even if she could find her voice, he wouldn't hear a thing she had to say.

"I'll wait up for you," she squeaked, sounding like the perfectly obedient wife.

"Don't," Shaw said, and by the look of him he knew it was perfectly clear to both of them where he would be sleeping that night.

"It's been nice meeting you," Brandy raised her voice for Marcus, who had walked out of the kitchen to give her a few minutes alone with Shaw.

"Yes, extremely charming." Marcus smiled at her. "I'll talk to you later."

"Goodbye, Uncle Marcus," Eric said from his place in front of the television set.

Shaw's scowl darkened, and Brandy thought, *he's jealous!* Just because Eric took to his brother more quickly than he had taken to Shaw. Brandy wanted to smooth her hand over Shaw's brow to assure him that to Eric, Shaw was still his hero. But he didn't give her the chance, and it would probably have angered him further if she had tried something so intimate in front of Marcus.

Brandy found it difficult to settle down that evening. The time was somewhat bearable while Eric was still awake and she could forget her fears by reading to him, playing with his toys and treating him to a special evening snack of homemade fudge. She would have kept him up later than usual, just to have his company and keep her thoughts of Shaw at bay, but the day in court, meeting Marcus and the full evening of playing with Brandy had worn him out. He was practically nodding off to sleep before she could tuck him between the covers.

What now? she asked herself, when it was only 9:30 and she was too keyed up to watch television or read a book, although she tried both. If it had not been for Eric asleep in the next room, she would have slipped out of the apartment just to go for a walk—anything to get away from Shaw. His presence was just as profound in the apartment when he was gone as it was when he was home.

She could smell the scent of him from his collection of toiletries, and his arrogance was stamped on his bold decorating. When she tried playing some of his records, she was reminded of his smoky, seductive green eyes laughing at her, enticing her into his arms.

It was after midnight when she finally crawled into bed, dressed in her most demure set of lounging pajamas—a jumpsuit. As she lay stiffly in bed, tensed for the sound of the door, she hoped Shaw would find gaining access to her body as difficult as opening the tin of a sardine can. She wished the outfit had feet sewn into it, but that would just irritate Shaw, and make it all the more difficult for her to pretend she despised his touch when, in fact, she found herself wanting him more and more each day.

The luminous dials of the clock read 3:46 when Shaw came in. He and Marcus were being very quiet tiptoeing around, and the carpet muffled most of the sounds. She heard movements in the kitchen where they were quietly talking. Dare she creep closer to the door to try to catch their conversation, she wondered? With her luck Shaw would open the bedroom door and she would fall into the living room. It was safer to lie here trying to guess what they were doing.

Then she heard the sound of running water in the bathroom next door. Of course, it could be Eric getting a drink of water in the middle of the night, but more than likely it was Marcus getting ready for his sofabed, for in the next instant the bedroom door opened and Shaw stood there, his feet spread apart, his body outlined by the soft backlighting of a lamp from the living room.

His hair was falling onto his forehead and she wondered why he stood there hesitating, surveying her and the bed like some kind of swarthy pirate about to ravage and plunder. All he needed was a sword in a sheath at his side to complete the picture, and mentally she drew it in, knowing he didn't need a weapon to force her to surrender.

She wanted him to take her. She wanted to taste his brand of lovemaking, because she already belonged to him body and soul. The problem was that he didn't love *her*. He just loved her body because it was the piece of candy she held out of his reach.

She must have called out his name, involuntarily, unable to deny the pain of her longing.

Just as he was about to turn away, he caught the

sound of his name and moved back into the room. "What?" He stepped closer, his eyes piercing the gloom of the room in the light straying from the living room. "I thought you were asleep."

Her heart was pounding. Was he just stopping in to check on her? Had he no intention of sliding into bed with her tonight when his brother would be sleeping on the couch? Surely that was the only reason Shaw had asked Marcus to visit—just so he would have an excuse to claim his rightful place in his bed.

"No," she whispered, unable to say anything else, for he was unknotting his tie now, stretching his neck as he unbuttoned the starched collar of his shirt. It filled her with delight just to watch these simple actions of his, to know that she was close enough to touch him.

He sat down at the edge of the bed, his thigh touching her knee through the coverlet. She could feel the heat of his body and smell the scent of him. He began pulling off his shoes, just as he must have done countless times, times when she hadn't lain here in his bed, times when he had been alone, or when some other woman had been in her place.

"Mind if I turn on the light?" he asked.

"No," she croaked, watching his powerfully muscled arm reach to the lamp switch on the night table beside her head. He stood up then and padded across the room, kicking the door shut with his toe as he began undoing his shirt, his face distracted, as if he were alone.

It would be this way if I weren't here, thought Brandy. He was so tired all he could think about was sleep. But his eyes caught hers and the look said he would be aware of her if she were sleeping ten miles instead of ten steps from him. "Mind if I sleep here tonight?" he asked, somewhat sarcastically, resenting the fact that he had to ask permission to use his own bed. "The couch is pretty cramped for sleeping."

Of course Brandy couldn't protest, especially with Marcus sleeping outside the door. They had to keep up appearances of a loving, honeymooning couple, even to close family, for Eric's sake. "If all you want to do is sleep—" She wanted to make her position clear.

"It's not all I *want* to do," he made his own desires explicit, "but it's all I intend to do at this point. I'm dead tired and I have no desire to have a hairpulling, backscratching fight at this hour of the morning. I can see it in your eyes—that's all I'd get if I so much as tried to kiss you goodnight."

Brandy's eyes rounded. She was wary of him, because she wanted him to make love to her, and she was afraid of what would happen when he did. But she also wanted him badly, and worried that her desire would show in her eyes.

He stripped off his shirt and threw it onto a chair. "I won't have to fight to get you," he reminded her. "When the time is right, we'll both know it. And you'll want me just as much as I want you. You'll come to me willingly enough."

"Don't hold your breath waiting," she told him, at the same time wondering herself how much longer she could resist touching him when he was so close.

"I'm going to take my pants off now, in case you want to look the other way," he grumbled.

Brandy turned away from him onto her side, and pulled the covers up closer to her chin.

She could hear all the sounds of his final undressing, the intimacy of being in such a position filling her with a breathlessness she could not control. She tensed as she felt him come up behind her. Would he haul her into his arms in spite of all his talk of her coming to him? Would he find her irresistible, even wearing this terry Winnie-the-Pooh-style outfit? Would he reach out and caress her as he had done the previous evening?

He turned out the bedside light, filling the room with shadows that seemed to make him closer to her than ever before. *When?* she asked herself. When would he take her in his arms and tell her he loved her?

"Move over." He nudged her back with his knee. "You're sleeping on my side of the bed."

Brandy scrambled to the extreme side of the bed. The nerve of the man! Treating her as if she were a cold fish! For two wooden nickels she'd show him she had a lot more to offer than whatever woman it was he spent most of his nights with. But maybe that was what he was counting on—making her angry enough to get her into his arms.

"Excuse me," she sniffed, "for trespassing."

"There's room enough for both of us. And you can even have this side if you like it so much. But you have to share it with me. I've had enough of that lumpy couch." She could hear his stretching. "This thing feels so good it can almost distract me from the thought of who's here with me."

"I certainly wouldn't be sharing your bed with you, Shaw Janus, if I had any choice in the matter."

"Oh?" He yawned. "Don't you have a choice in the matter? You should be able to tell now that this thing is big enough for two people to sleep in without having to come into contact with each other at all. If that's what you want," he added as an afterthought. "I think you'll also admit it's a lot more comfortable than that overstuffed sofa out there. One thing it's taught me is never to buy anything on looks anymore—from sofas to wives."

Brandy gritted her teeth. "If you must sleep in this bed, you don't have to insult me. Believe me, if there was anything I could do about it, we wouldn't both be in this bed right now."

"If that's how you feel about it," his voice was lazy over a long yawn, "then find somewhere else to sleep. I don't care."

"And where for heaven's sake?"

"Try the couch." He turned over, his back to her as if to put an end to their discussion.

"Oh, you'd like that, wouldn't you? It'd give you an excuse to accuse me of being unfaithful—sleeping with your brother. Well, no thanks."

He yawned before he answered.

"Marcus isn't here."

"He isn't?" Brandy sat up in bed, dragging the covers with her. "Where is he? I thought I heard him in the bathroom."

"Must have been Eric," he mumbled.

"You mean, he's not spending the night here?"

"No. He thought he'd go to a hotel and give us a little newlywed privacy. He likes to write it off on his expense account, and a hotel gives him some privacy, too."

"But—but—"

"Yes?"

"Then why did you have me make up the couch for a bed?"

"Because," he turned back over and she could imagine him lying with his hand behind his head, watching her, even though he couldn't see her, in the dark, "I thought you probably wouldn't like the idea of sharing my bed, and I'm tired of sleeping out there."

She wanted to smother him with a pillow, but any move she made toward him would just have him laughing at her. She was tempted to stay in his bed to prove him wrong, but she knew that while he wouldn't touch her at that moment since he was taking such pleasure in making fun of her, she couldn't trust his aloofness to last through to morning. If she uttered another word, she might end up doing something she would regret.

"It's probably not half as lumpy as you think it is." She scrambled out of bed, dragging the coverlet with her.

"Oh, no." He grabbed at the covers. "My bedding stays with my bed, which, I'll say again, you're welcome to share."

"No, thank you," she said primly.

"I thought as much." He turned over again, his body cocooning itself into the coverlet so that she couldn't jerk it out from underneath him. "Then enjoy the lumps and that scratchy blanket that goes with it."

Brandy jerked the bedroom door open, prepared to slam it behind her.

"I wouldn't." He read her thoughts. "You might wake Eric. Oh, and Brandy?"

"What?" she pouted at him from the doorway.

"I'd like poached eggs for breakfast if you know how to cook them."

"Ice water down the back is more what you deserve," she fumed, as she heard him snickering behind her.

Brandy awoke the next morning to the smell of coffee. It smelled so strong and near, she imagined she could feel the heat of the liquid, and when she opened her eyes it was to see Shaw smiling at her, his face on a level with hers on the bed of the couch, a cup of coffee offered in his hands.

"Lumpy, isn't it?" he asked.

She moved to a sitting position, wondering how she had gotten any sleep at all trying to find a comfortable way to curl up on the sectional sofa. She kept falling into the cracks between the sections, and the humps of stuffing were all rounded out of shape with the way her body, and Shaw's, were built. "Oh, it's not so bad." She clutched her side suddenly as she became aware of a crick in her back.

"If you say so." His eyes laughed at her. He handed her the coffee cup. "Care to spend another night here?"

"I might move in with Eric." She sipped the hot coffee, trying to ignore him casually sitting down beside her, dressed in his thick terry robe, his hair still wet from the shower.

"You could move in with me." He slanted his eyes at her. "You'd be surprised how amicable I can be when I get a good night's sleep."

"I don't think I'd get much sleep with you in that bed."

"Oh?" His eyebrows shot up. "So you admit it makes you hot with desire just thinking about sharing that bed? I thought you'd come to see things my way."

"You're deliberately misunderstanding me," she accused, not yet awake enough to fight his word games.

His face relaxed. "Yes, I admit I am, but no longer.

Last night was the only way I could think of for getting my bed back. And I'll tell you one thing for certain right now, young lady, I spent my last night on this couch two nights ago. I'm moving back into my bed, and you're welcome to share it with me if you like."

"You know I can't do that."

"Can't? Or won't?"

She pretended an absorption with her coffee cup to avoid answering.

"I won't bite you know. I meant what I said. I will not force myself on you. You have my word as a gentleman on that."

"But we both know you're not a gentleman."

"I could be." His brows shot up. "You're having a surprisingly mellow effect on me, whether you realize it or not. Look," he said, taking the cup out of her hands and setting it on the table. "I've agreed to help you gain custody of Eric. Yesterday should have proved to you how much I mean to help you."

She nodded, grudgingly.

"Well," he took her hand in his own, holding them in his lap, "shouldn't we present a united front to help Eric?"

"There are limits to what I'll do for appearances sake. Especially when it means sharing your bed when no one can see."

"All I'm saying is there's no reason we both have to be miserable. There's no reason why we shouldn't both share that comfortable bed in there—just for sleeping."

Brandy eyed him warily, wishing it were so simple.

He stared up at the ceiling, realizing he wasn't getting through to her. "What do I have to do to convince you?" He turned his eyes to her, piercing her with his sincerity. "Don't you know by now I could have come in there any night since we've been married? You can never lock any doors to me. And I'm stronger than you. It would be so easy to take you. But I've given you my word I won't until I know you're equally willing."

Brandy looked down. He was making her feel guilty.

He touched her chin and turned her face to him. "Let me tell you something, my innocent little wife. If I wanted to make love to you, I sure wouldn't hold my passion in check until I could find a bed."

Brandy blushed at the expression in his eyes. From the depths of her she knew the strength he had to arouse her. She was wanting him all over again, right now, right here. She closed her eyes and hoped it wasn't too late, before he had read that desire.

He leaned over and gently kissed her cheek. "Why don't we try being friends for a change and see where that gets us?"

"I'd like that," said Brandy, wanting to trust him with her body and soul, because she realized he had become her life. He was being so gentle this morning, so compassionate. This time it was directed at her.

"Good." He held out his hand. "Let's shake on it."

Brandy took his hand and thanked him with her eyes. The last few weeks had been such a strain worrying what he would do when they were alone. "Poached eggs, wasn't it?"

His eyes crinkled in amusement. "I was only teasing. A bowl of cereal will suffice."

"Oh, no." She smiled. "Your wish is my command. At least as far as breakfast is concerned," she added, seeing the delight that flared in his eyes.

"Such is my luck," he muttered good humoredly.

"It could change," she tossed over her shoulder as she went into the kitchen to see what sort of feast she could prepare.

Chapter Nine

True to his word, Shaw steered clear of Brandy. He even stopped taunting her with his speech. She realized she owed half of her luck to the fact that he was seldom in the apartment. His excuse was the last minute details of the opening for his new restaurant, but Brandy thought more than likely he was attending to the details of another woman. Although he was discreet, it didn't stop her jealousy.

Still, the lack of interest in her at night showed her a new side to Shaw's personality. How he could sleep with her so close to him was beyond her; she would lie awake for hours listening to the sound of his breathing, content just in knowing he was beside her. She longed to feel his arms around her, holding her through the night. It must be one of the special joys of marriage, she thought, a tear slipping from her eye, whenever she remembered she didn't really have a marriage at all— She was a married single. A piece of paper said they were legally married, but it didn't guarantee they would have a marriage, nor did the fact that Eric was asleep in the next room. The fact that Brandy had married Shaw for the sake of a child did not mean that child could hold them together.

Legalities, children, and desire did not make a marriage: only love would guarantee a marriage survival, and Brandy had little hope that Shaw would ever feel that for her.

Eric seemed to have a softening effect on Shaw. Though Shaw spent little time at the apartment, the time he was there he spent primarily engaged in entertaining the boy. Brandy watched them together as she prepared dinner. She thought that Shaw would make a wonderful father some day, if only he would give some woman the chance to give him children.

He had just that amount of dominance to let Eric know he couldn't get away with things, and he had just that amount of frivolity to make him fun to be with. As each day slipped into the next, Brandy found that she was not only jealous of Shaw spending his nights at the restaurant, but also envious of the amount of time he spent with Eric. She wished he would show her half the attention he showed the boy, but to be fair, Brandy knew Eric needed it much more than she did. The kind of attention Shaw would show her, if she gave him half a chance, was not the kind she needed if she were eventually to get an annulment.

Still, it pleased her immensely when Shaw telephoned her one afternoon to tell her they would be attending a party that evening. He had already arranged for a babysitter for Eric, and wanted to be certain she had something appropriate to wear.

"What kind of a party is it?" she asked.

"You might call it a get acquainted party. My *friends* want to get to know you." He didn't sound too happy, and she wondered if he were ashamed to have others in his circle meet her. "Believe me, if there was any way I could get out of it, I would."

"Oh," said Brandy, trying to ignore his displeasure, and think of what she could wear to impress his friends. She had worn glamorous clothes modeling, but had never saved enough money to own such finery. Shaw gave her carte blanche to run out and buy something, but pride would not let her spend his money so extravagantly.

Instead, she remembered a local designer whose clothes she had modeled shortly after coming to Atlanta. The woman had liked the way Brandy looked in the dresses so much that she had offered to loan her some of her special creations whenever Brandy needed, on the premise that it was good advertising. Whenever anyone asked her where she had bought the clothes, she would tell them about the designer.

Brandy called Candace James immediately. After explaining about the party, she asked Candace if she could come down and look at a dress.

"By all means," said Candace, remembering Brandy's petite, shapely frame and already deciding on the kind of dress she wanted her to wear. "I could use a little word-of-mouth advertising right now, and who could be better than Shaw Janus's wife? Whenever did you get married?"

Brandy laughed and told her, making it all sound as though she were still the blushing bride. In fact, it embarrassed her to tell people, because she could just imagine what they would be saying in a few months when she and Shaw got an annulment.

Candace, her mouth full of pins, met Brandy at the door of her studio an hour later. "Come in, come in," she mumbled. "I'm just sticking together some different materials to see what effect I might get—I'm working with contrasts for the next season. Come, I picked out two or three things for you to choose from."

"I was hoping you wouldn't mind," said Brandy, "and also praying that you wouldn't have forgotten who I was."

"I never forget a pretty face." She winked. "Especially since you have the exact kind of figure I have in mind when I'm designing. Many women these days are *not* tall and thin. Shorter women, I find, since I am one myself, have a hard time finding a selection of clothes."

Brandy nodded. There were usually two or three size sixes and fewer size threes whenever she shopped for clothes. That was another reason she had trouble with modeling: most designer dresses came in sevens and eights, so there were not that many standard sizes she could wear and show off to advantage at the same time.

"That's why I like my clothes to really stand out," Candace continued, "but subtly, not with a lot of gaudy spangles and fringe. Subtlety, like a woman's size, can very often be very provocative. Here." She showed Brandy the selection she had laid out.

Brandy's hands went immediately to a dress of crepe material in a pattern of large pastel watercolor flowers on a white background. A violet sash, the dress's only accent, tied it into a shirtwaist; the long sleeves ended in narrow cuffs at her wrists; the below-the-knee length skirt could show off her tanned legs by leaving a few buttons undone.

"Try it on," Candace urged. "I thought that one would be perfect for you, but I laid out the two others to give you somewhat of a choice."

She stood back and admired how her work shown to advantage against Brandy's dark, curly hair. "Perfect. It even looks expensive by the way you carry your body. Good . . . good." She watched Brandy walk. "Pretend a string is pulling you up from the back of the head. If your spine is correct, everything else will fall right into place. And whatever you do, don't lean on one hip—it looks tacky and outdated these days."

Brandy laughed at her charm school lesson. Fondling the dress as if it were a present, a precious one that Shaw might have given her, she said, "I shouldn't have called you, Candace. You're taking an awful responsibility letting me borrow this. What if I spill something on it?"

"Don't," Candace warned, then laughed, "because I'm saving it for myself, but it looks a lot better on you than I ever even imagined it would on me. Wear it in good health, and be sure everybody knows where it came from."

Brandy laughed. "Will do."

"But—" Candace was looking rather critically at the dress, and then she stepped forward and unbuttoned all the fastenings to the bodice. "Get rid of the bra and wear it open to the waist. The buttons are just decoration. I shouldn't have even put buttonholes in it."

She loosened the waist sash and pulled the open front of the shirtwaist together. "Let me pin this here." She made an alteration, then retied the sash in place. "There

. . . that's better. A little more decent, yet sensual because the buttons are still obviously afly."

Brandy blushed. "Couldn't I just—one button?"

"No," said Candace. "Ruins the whole effect. It's not that bad. Go look in the mirror."

Brandy did as she was told and had to admit she didn't look *that* undressed. But what would Shaw say when he saw it?

Fortunately, Brandy didn't see Shaw until the last minute. He was running so late with last minute work at his business that he arranged for Marcus to drive to the apartment and pick up Brandy while he changed at his office.

Marcus didn't comment when he saw Brandy, nor did he talk much on the drive to the suburban mansion where the festivities were taking place. Both wondered what Shaw's reaction would be when he saw Brandy.

The house, at the end of a long, wooded, sweeping drive, was a great English Tudor mansion. When Brandy asked, Marcus was closemouthed about the house's owners, merely stating that it was the home of a friend of Shaw's. From the way he said "friend," Brandy assumed it was a girlfriend.

"Well, everybody seems to be here already," Marcus commented, parking the car far down the drive and getting out to help Brandy.

Brandy's palms sweated. It was almost as if she, Shaw's wife, had been invited as an afterthought, yet it was the party's purpose to introduce her. It also didn't help that she noticed the party was in full progress, and had been long before she was told to arrive. She didn't say a word to Marcus as he took her hand and steadied her out of the car. She was glad now she hadn't run out and bought something to try to compete with the other women who would be here this evening. If she had, she would have felt too self-conscious spending the kind of money she'd need for a dress in their league. Wearing a Candace James original would be prestigious enough, and it would show in the way she carried herself.

Brandy and Marcus walked up the drive to the sound of laughter and live music. Who was paying for this extravaganza? Brandy wondered.

"Marcus." Brandy held back as he was about to ring the door bell.

He looked down, his eyes dark and smoldering the way Shaw's could when he was angry.

"I'm frightened," she whispered. "I don't know anyone in there."

"You know me." He smiled, but like Shaw, the smile didn't reach his eyes. "And you know Shaw, if he can spare the time for you," he muttered. He squeezed her arm. "You look beautiful, Brandy. That should give you confidence enough. I have a feeling you'll be able to hold your own this evening, but if you get worried about that, just look across the room for me. I'll be there watching out for you, if you need me."

Brandy relaxed beneath his look. She knew he was being sincere, and it was nice to know she had an ally.

The door opened to a glittering hallway with a curving staircase swirling to the upper levels of the house. It seemed out of place with the outside facade, almost fake, but the amount of money that had been spent on the single crystal chandelier spoke of riches beyond Brandy's imagination.

Brandy stepped with Marcus across the mosaic tiled floor into the living area where the majority of the guests were congregating. She tightened the muscles in her stomach, remembering her modeling training, and decided that to boost her confidence she would pretend she was modeling. She held her rib cage high, her shoulders back, and her spine straight as she put one foot in front of the other and entered the room.

Seeing men notice her entrance and turn to look at her made her relax—she knew several gave Marcus envious glances.

Brandy looked for Shaw, but didn't see him. She did, however, notice the man he had lunched with the day at Peachtree Plaza. It was hard to miss him, especially when he bellowed out to the group that Shaw's wife had arrived.

Brandy was soon surrounded by wellwishers and anxious young men eager for an excuse to kiss the bride. Marcus drifted away from her side, and she soon realized she could stand on her own, and more than that, was actually enjoying the attention. Perhaps, she thought, if so many other men were eager for her company Shaw would realize what a prize he had in Brandy.

Laughing and chatting, she allowed those she met to lead her around and introduce her to various business-men and prominent citizens of the community, but all the while kept a lookout for Shaw; it seemed odd that strangers were making the introductions instead of her own husband.

Someone brought her a glass of champagne and several in the crowd toasted to her. The champagne felt bubbly going down, but the quickness of her swallow-ing made tears well behind her eyes. *Where is Shaw?* she wondered. Had he even arrived? Did he prefer having a private party with someone else in some other room of the mansion? She emptied her glass and found it just as quickly replaced by another.

Take it easy, she warned herself. She had to be prepared for whatever games Shaw was playing. It was as if she were on display, yet he didn't seem proud enough to be the one to show her off to his friends. She had been forced to arrive with Shaw's brother. She had no choice but to shuffle from person to person making small talk about subjects she was only vaguely aware. Perhaps this was another of Shaw's games—giving her enough rope to hang herself by saying the wrong thing to his best friends.

Finally Shaw appeared, although she concluded that he had arrived a long time ago. She vowed not to let her frustration show, as she noted a tall woman beside him, her hand on his arm—a rather possessive hand at that, Brandy thought. She recognized the woman as the evening hostess at Shaw's restaurant and she had wondered from the beginning what other relationship the two might have.

It was plainly obvious as the other woman's eyes caught Brandy's that she was laying prior claim to Brandy's husband. It didn't help that everyone in the room greeted the woman as one of their own.

Brandy watched Shaw shake hands with many of the guests, the woman sticking close by his side. *He doesn't even have the decency to set that woman aside and take the hand of his own wife*, Brandy thought angrily.

But the next moment Brandy remembered her place —she was Shaw's wife and a stranger in the midst of Shaw's longtime business associates and friends. She also remembered something else—he was her husband. That was what this stupid party was all about anyway! If he didn't want everyone to know the fact of their marriage, he should never have agreed to let the party be in their honor.

"Excuse me," Brandy said to the woman she had been speaking to, "but I see my husband has just come in. I've so enjoyed meeting you and hope we get a chance to chat later."

Brandy walked determinedly up to Shaw and his companion, daring the woman to keep her arm on Shaw in her presence. Brandy's eyes glared as the woman let her hand slip away from Shaw's jacket-clad arm.

"Hello," said Brandy, holding out her hand to the man Shaw was talking to. "I'm Brandy Janus."

"Well, hello." The man's eyes lit up and he turned his full attention to Brandy. "You didn't tell me Marcus had gotten married," the man said over his shoulder to Shaw, while his eyes devoured Brandy.

"He didn't," Brandy informed him. "Shaw did." She slid into position between the woman and Shaw, clutching his arm even more possessively than the other girl had.

Shaw looked at her—and then all the way down her open front—and the expression in his eyes was not one of his most pleasant. Snuggling closer, Brandy smiled up at him, further wedging her body into his and the other woman out of the conversation. Brandy felt the muscles in her neck knotting with tension and anger; she had sat home night after night waiting for him, hoping he would come home just to talk to her, if nothing else, and all the while he had probably been with his hostess. Before Brandy could elaborate on their marriage, Shaw was excusing them and hustling Brandy out of the room.

"We can't leave now," Brandy protested, knowing there was safety in numbers, and afraid of a confrontation with Shaw.

"To hell with the party," he said. "This was not my idea."

"It wasn't?" Brandy hung behind, making it difficult for him to push her further. "You can't think I arranged it. I don't know any of your friends."

"In a way you did, though." He glared, taking her resisting wrist and hauling her onto the terrace.

"Me? How?" She stumbled after him.

"My whole life has changed since you entered it!"

"Do you think mine hasn't also?"

"That's different. You're a woman."

"Oh," Brandy fumed, shaking her wrist free of his touch. "Since when have you taken a dislike to women? Certainly not tonight the way that blonde was cutting off the circulation in your arm! Everybody noticed."

"So what? Most of them know her. Nobody knows you."

"Is that my fault?"

"Yes." He lowered his face to her level.

"I thought you were going to try to be discreet with your affairs until all this mess with Eric was settled, but I guess it was too much to trust you to care about him."

"It's because I care about him that I'm in this blasted mess. And it's because of him that this idiotic nuptial party is taking place tonight."

"How?" she challenged.

"Because Lorraine saw the thing in the paper about our custody battle and, of course, the little fact that we were recently married. I'd been hoping to keep it from *her*, of all people."

Brandy tapped her toe on the flagstones. "I can see that it would make it easier to keep your little affair going if she were in the dark about your marriage."

Shaw's eyes widened, and Brandy cringed. She'd said

too much that time, but luckily he had enough self-control not to resort to violence.

"We are not now having an affair," he said through gritted teeth.

"Then why did you invite her to this party?"

"I didn't invite her," he said slowly and distinctly. "She invited us. All of us. This is her home. It was all her stupid idea to have everyone get to know you . . . especially her."

"But I don't understand." She frowned. "Why would she want to give *us* a party if she and you still—"

"We aren't *still*—" he paused for emphasis, "and the reason she gave this party is because she knows how much I *hate* this kind of thing."

"Oh," said Brandy, as if she understood, but she was more confused than ever. One thing was becoming clear, however, and that was that Shaw was no more happy to be here than she was. "Why don't we leave then?"

"We can't leave!" He stomped away from her in exasperation. "We're the guests of honor."

"I suppose that's why you had Marcus bring me . . . why you couldn't bring me yourself."

"I didn't bring you because I've been tied up with the details of opening the restaurant, but I can see I should have brought you—if for no other reason than to make you wear something more decent than that dress." He stepped back to her and began buttoning up the dress.

She put her hands over his. "It's supposed to be worn open."

"Who says?"

"The designer." She undid all the buttons.

"Well, your husband says it should be buttoned up all the way to the throat."

"No." She argued.

He lifted his eyes to the porch ceiling. "Why is it whenever we're out in public you let every man near you see more of your body than I can when you're lying in bed with me? How come *I* always get left out?"

"It's not that I'm trying to leave you out," Brandy tried to explain. "It's just that—" She wasn't finding it easy to tell him how she felt. "Let's go home," she said instead.

Shaw grasped her shoulders, his eyes blazing with emotion. "Why do you always tell me things like that when it's impossible to do anything about it?"

"Because," she involuntarily licked her lower lip, "it's safer that way."

"Oh, baby." His eyes softened as they concentrated on her full, moist lips. "Why are you so afraid of me?"

"Shaw," she said, her hands going to the front of his white shirt, smoothing over the material beneath his jacket. "You're so experienced . . . and I'm not . . . not at all. How can I satisfy you? How can I compare to women like her?"

He pulled her closer, chuckling at her fears, holding her loosely in his arms as he cuddled her next to his chest. "You wouldn't be half so special if you tried to compete with everyone else. You're unique, like no other woman I've known. That's why you're so dear to me."

Brandy's heart was fluttering like a captive butterfly. He sounded so tender, so sincere, and the words were honey to her ears. She stared up at him. Was he just saying these things because he knew it was what she wanted to hear? Or did he mean them?

She didn't take time to think any longer as his lips came down on hers and she was swallowed up in sensations that she thought must be love. It was what she wanted to feel from Shaw, and she wouldn't question it any longer. It was enough now to take what she could get from him for as long as it lasted. She had trapped him into marriage, perhaps she could snare him into loving her as well. She knew now that was what she wanted, why she had been so determined all along in choosing him for her husband. She wanted to love Shaw and have him love her back. To be his wife and have him as her husband—not for Eric's sake, but for her own. She couldn't help loving him. Perhaps if she were with him long enough, he wouldn't be able to resist loving her, either.

She responded to his kiss with all the love in her heart. She had to show him her love since to voice the words would only make him angry and send him away from her.

He moaned against her cheek, "I'd give anything if we could slip away from here—just to be alone for a couple of hours."

"Yes," said Brandy, his words exciting her. She was committed to this man. He was her husband. She wanted to be a wife to him in every way. She could feel him wavering between desire and obligation. She ran her hands around his chest to his back, snuggling closer inside his loose jacket. She wanted to hide in Shaw rather than face again that roomful of strangers—people who were Shaw's friends, but not her own. They were the type of people who speared olives at cocktail parties and at the same time stabbed backs, she thought.

She shuddered involuntarily at the thought. Shaw hugged her closer. "We'll stay just long enough to have another drink or two," he decided, "and meanwhile you stay in the mood you're in right now."

"I won't promise," said Brandy, disappointed that she wasn't getting her way right this minute. Still, leaving early with Shaw was better than closing the party down, or having him leave with someone else.

He seared her mouth with another breathless kiss that weakened her knees and left her standing docilely in front of him as he buttoned up the bodice of her dress.

As she went back to the party with Shaw, Brandy felt much stronger. This time she was arriving with him beside her, making a grander entrance than before. They were husband and wife, and she wanted everyone to see how hard it was for them to keep their eyes, and hands, off each other.

Shaw was very attentive to Brandy, even drinking a toast to her with champagne instead of his usual Scotch. They linked arms like lovers and tried to swallow their drinks without spilling them while giggling at the absurdity of their honeymoon games. Lorraine had bought a large wedding cake topped with a bride and groom and Shaw went through the motions of gaily cutting the cake with Brandy, even smearing a slice of cake around her pretty lips to the delight of the guests. But Brandy didn't care, for his eyes were teasing, and at the same time anticipatory. Little did the guests know that night would actually be their true wedding night.

Brandy enjoyed herself, and despite the fact that all the guests were strangers to her, she was gracious and friendly. Shaw was beside her, and that was all that mattered. She even forgot about Marcus watching her from the background, ready to come to her aid should she need a little extra confidence.

"How long have you been married?" Everyone wanted to know. Shaw would answer with a knowing look at Brandy, "She swept me off my feet. I hardly knew what was happening."

All the while Lorraine was hovering in the background, playing the role of the perfect hostess, trying to assert her relationship with Shaw whenever she had the opportunity.

Brandy couldn't relax with her near. Whenever Lorraine sidled up to Shaw, Brandy tried to slip away, but he would ensnare her wrist and break his contact with Lorraine.

As hard as Brandy tried to ignore her, Lorraine finally got her chance alone with her. Brandy slipped away to the ladies' room, her head reeling from the countless glasses of champagne, and Lorraine followed her.

Brandy sat down at the vanity table, wishing her head would clear and her hand steady as she touched up her makeup. But as Lorraine came into the room behind her, Brandy was thankful for the haze the alcohol gave her. It made it easier to face Lorraine.

The other woman ran a brush through her hair, as if it were truly a coincidence that they happened to be in the ladies' room at the same moment.

"You won't get away with it," Lorraine said without preamble, tugging at her blonde locks.

Brandy didn't answer: she couldn't trust herself to. She was afraid if she tried to respond, Lorraine would have a quicker wit, so she sat silently, outlining her lips with a lipstick pencil, enraging Lorraine because she was ignoring her.

"He only married you for *one* reason, you know," Lorraine continued. "As soon as he tires of you he'll come back to me."

Brandy dug in her makeup kit for her lipstick.

Lorraine pried deeper. "Once he sees how much more satisfying a woman with experience is, you won't be able to keep him. He's already spending more time with me than he is at home with you."

Brandy wanted to argue, her neck muscles tightening again at the tension between them, but she knew she didn't have a defense. Just because Shaw spent time away from home didn't necessarily mean he was spending all that time with Lorraine—maybe he really *was* busy at work on the restaurant. For the first time she hoped that were true, but a quick glance in Lorraine's direction said it wasn't probable. The woman *was* beautiful and experienced.

"And what do you have to offer him?" Lorraine continued with her monologue.

Brandy turned to face her. "Love."

Lorraine laughed. "He can have *that* with any number of women. That's funny if you think you can hold him with something as tenuous as that."

"It's the *only* thing that will hold us together," said Brandy, knowing it was the truth, but also that Shaw had to love her as much as she loved him for the marriage to work. "He can have the entire female population, but I don't think anyone's ever offered him love before."

"My, but you're such an innocent. Money's much more important to Shaw than love; I guess you haven't known him long enough to have figured that out. He needs money to make this new restaurant of his a success and *I* can give him the money."

"He'll be a success because of the person he is, not because he has to hold onto the apron strings of some rich snob."

Lorraine's face darkened. "If you love him, you'll let him go. The restaurant means the world to him. I'll see that he doesn't get the money he needs if you stay with him. Without that money he'll be broken financially. There are a lot of expenses involved with a venture of this size and it's a gamble for any man. Shaw has me and my money as the ace in the hole, but not for much longer, lady—not if you persist in your notions of love and marriage."

"You can't threaten me," said Brandy calmly, putting her makeup back in her purse to hide her shaking hands.

"Threaten you?" Lorraine laughed. "I'm not threatening you, sweetheart. I'm merely telling it to you like it is. Without me, Shaw will be a failure—and I don't think you want that for him. Just ask him sometime how important that restaurant is to him. He already owes my father quite a bit of money. All I have to do is see that father doesn't let him borrow anymore."

"Shaw is not the kind of man to stoop to your petty style of blackmail." Brandy faced Lorraine. "If he can't get the money from you, he'll get it elsewhere. Shaw's a prominent man in town. It shouldn't be too hard."

"Don't count on it," Lorraine spat. "He also has quite a reputation, which should also look good if it were brought out in this ridiculous custody battle you've involved him in."

Brandy's hair hid her face, as she brushed it all forward vigorously to keep from showing her fears, then she tossed it all back, her eyes shining as she faced Lorraine squarely for the last time. She couldn't sit there any longer and put up with Lorraine's spitefulness. "You seem to forget one thing. Shaw married *me*. That speaks a lot more strongly than the kind of relationship the two of you shared—in the past. It's a lot more binding. And if you're so concerned about Shaw's success with the restaurant, you'd do well to tell him of your threats to withdraw your money. He and I don't *ever* discuss business. Now, if you'll excuse me, my *husband* is waiting for me." She stood up, forcing her legs to walk out of the room rather than bolt like a frightened lamb. If she listened to Lorraine much longer she knew she'd be weeping.

Chapter Ten

The drive home was an unusually quiet one: on Shaw's side as he contemplated the seduction of his wife, and on Brandy's as she wondered whether she could let him make love to her. She had to give Lorraine credit for choosing the worst time to make Brandy feel guilty about her deception of Shaw. If she continued this charade—if only for Eric's sake—would it ruin Shaw's personal and business life?

"Shaw," she said as they neared the apartment.

"Hmmm?" He smiled across at her and reached out to take her hand in his own.

"How important is this new restaurant to you?"

"Do you need to ask?"

She frowned. "Yes."

He shrugged, stroking her hand as best as he could while driving at the same time. "It's my first step in the big business world. Without this second restaurant I'm nothing more than a glorified manager, and never will be anything more."

"I don't understand."

"The first restaurant was just a piece of a franchise that's operating all over the country. I'm opening the new place based on the reputation I've made with The Pub, but it's my restaurant this time. I won't answer to anyone, nor have to share any of the profits. That's why the White Horse Pub means so much to me," he explained honestly.

She nodded, beginning to understand. "And you've put a lot of money into it?"

"Just about everything," he admitted, "but you shouldn't worry about that. We're going to be a big success."

Brandy prayed that would be true. "But what if something happened? What if you didn't get all the money you needed to open the White Horse Pub?"

"I don't even want to think like that. Negative thinking is the beginning of a person's downfall to my way of thinking. We're *going* to succeed."

Any other time, Brandy would have taken some delight in the way he said "we" as if he were including her . . . but whether he knew it or not, she was part of the venture—perhaps the key to his succeeding or failing, if Lorraine's words were true.

"Are you going to have to borrow a lot of money?"

"Hey—" He looked across at her. "I feel like I'm taking home my bank manager instead of my wife . . . and tonight of all nights I'd rather *not* talk business."

If only it were that simple, Brandy thought, quietly

brooding over his words for the rest of the way back to
the apartment. He noticed her silence as he opened the
door, but only smiled, thinking she was looking ahead
to their time together in bed.

Brandy checked on Eric while Shaw paid the babysitter and escorted her outside to her car. Eric was
sound asleep, content in his new home. How much
longer would they remain here? Brandy wondered.

Would he be allowed to stay long enough to wake up
here in the morning? Or would Shaw dismiss them from
the apartment as he had the babysitter once he knew
the truth about his marriage to Brandy? She *had* to tell
him. If they were to have any kind of marriage at all, it
had to begin with honesty. She had told him weeks ago
that if he cared enough about Eric, then nothing
Brandy could do to Shaw should interfere with his
feelings for the boy.

She was so wrapped up in her thoughts she didn't
hear him enter the apartment and walk softly across the
deep pile carpet. The next thing she knew he was
standing beside her, his hands on her shoulders, looking at Eric with her. Brandy closed her eyes. She
wanted so much to share children with Shaw—not just
Eric, but other little boys and girls that she could give
him. But after she told him the truth, she might not
even know the touch of his lovemaking.

He kissed the side of her neck, and nibbled at her
ear. "You're looking in on Eric the same way I've
looked in on you each night when you were sleeping
alone in my bed." His breath was warm against her
neck.

"You mean you came in and watched me sleeping?"

"No." His lips trailed up her cheek as his hands came
around to cross in front of her and hold her closer

against him. "I only trusted myself as far as the door. The other night I was turning away, resigning myself to another night on the couch, when I realized you were awake. And then I couldn't resist laying in bed with you."

Brandy trembled in his arms at the intensity of his caring. She knew he could have entered the bedroom any time he wanted to, but had not: She realized it was out of respect for her that he had endured the lumps of the couch.

"Now, more than ever, I can't wait to take you to my bed the way I should have done weeks ago. You're ready, aren't you?"

"Yes, but—"

"Shhh." His lips silenced her. "You don't need words any longer, Brandy. It's the least effective means of communication between a man and a woman."

"But you don't understand—"

"I think I do." His lips trailed down her neck, as he quietly shut Eric's door.

"Shaw, I have to talk to you. I have to explain."

He ignored her, picking her up in his arms to carry her into the bedroom.

"Shaw—" She lay beneath him, unresisting as he began to undress her. "I don't know what to do."

"It'll all come back to you." He undid the last button of her dress and began unfastening his tie.

"No, it won't, because I've never made love to a man. Not even to you."

He tossed his tie aside and began unbuttoning his shirt. "Instinct will tell you what to do, even if you were too drunk to realize what happened between us on our wedding night."

"That's just the point. Nothing happened."

He was about to shrug off his shirt when the meaning of her words sank in. Shaw focused on her as Brandy continued, "You were the only one who was drunk, so drunk you don't even remember marrying me, so drunk all you could do when we got to the hotel room was to undress and fall into bed."

He frowned, trying to recapture the fragments of memory he had left from that night. "But the next morning—"

"I know." She looked down, unable to face him any longer. "I made it look like you had seduced me, but you hadn't. You've never even seen me—naked."

"Do you mean to tell me," his face flushed as realization flooded over him, "that all this time I've been feeling guilty for nothing? That there was absolutely no reason for me not to immediately get an annulment—and still isn't, for that matter?"

Brandy nodded. "No reason except whatever you might feel for Eric."

"Damn!" he said, throwing down his shirt as if it were a poisonous snake he was ready to flog to death. "And now," he glared at her, "I suppose you're telling me this as a last resort to keep me out of your bed again." He laughed. "Well, it won't work. I didn't marry you for nothing, lady, and if I have to be married to you for Eric's sake, I intend to get a few benefits out of the bargain."

Brandy didn't cringe from him as he expected she would. She loved Shaw and wanted him any way she could get him. If nothing else, she would have a memory to live with long after the marriage was dissolved. She might not ever be able to marry again after this night, but she didn't care. Shaw was the only man for her, and she felt it would be that way the rest of her life.

"Well?" He put one knee onto the bed.

"Well what?" She blinked up at him.

"Aren't you going to kick and scream?"

"No." She shook her head. "I was hoping you wouldn't change your mind after I told you, but I felt I had to tell you, to start our marriage out honestly."

He frowned, and Brandy added in a soft voice, "I want you to make love to me, Shaw, because I want to be married to you."

He scratched the hair on his chest, his eyes darkening. "Why?"

Brandy reached out and touched his knee, wishing she could effect a more intimate touch, as she said, "I love you, Shaw."

He hesitated, torn between his desire and his sense of principles, and then took two steps away from the bed muttering to himself. "Well, that just cuts it all," he flung over his shoulder to her. "You win! You finally win!"

"Win what?" Brandy propped on her elbow in bed, hoping her half-dressed appearance would be enough to lure him back to her.

"You win! I wouldn't make love to you now if you were the last female in town."

"Why not?" she wailed. "A minute ago you couldn't wait to get your hands on me!"

A look at his eyes told her his desire had not lessened, but that his mind had a strong influence over his body. "I told you not to fall in love with me. It always gums up a fine relationship between a man and a woman."

"I see it more as completing a relationship," Brandy said calmly.

"What would you know about such things?" He rummaged in his closet for a robe and pulled it over his shoulders. "You're just a little more than half my age. You've never even been with a man." He looked up at the ceiling, realizing again the full consequence of that fact. "But I've been around."

"Maybe it's time you settled down," she said, sitting up in bed now, still deliberately not bothering to alter all the undoing Shaw had already done to her clothes.

"With you I suppose?" He raked a hand through his hair.

"You could do worse . . . with somebody like Lorraine."

"Leave her out of it."

"How can I," she demanded, "when you spend every night with her? What kind of a husband do you call yourself?"

"No kind." His eyebrows lowered over his eyes. "Not now, not ever. And maybe that's something you need to realize, little lady. I've always been a bachelor. I'll always be one, and a little teenager like you isn't going to change that overnight."

"The bodies change," said Brandy softly, "but the act never does. Wouldn't it be better to build something worthwhile with one person?"

"For other people, maybe. For you, maybe. For me, no."

"Why not? You haven't even given it a try."

"There's a reason for that." He pulled the sash of his robe tighter. "I had the perfect example in my father. He was married four times, each ending in divorce. I'm a lot like him, but at least I have sense enough not to start something I know I can't finish . . . and marriage heads the top of that list."

"Up to now, anyway," said Brandy.

"Up to and including now." He made it clear.

"What are you going to do, Shaw, about Eric?"

"I'll live up to my bargain about him. To all outside appearances we'll be the happily married couple for as long as it takes. I can guarantee, though, you'll be safe from me in bed."

How could she tell him that was the last thing she wanted now? How could she show him how much she cared for him and wanted to make a life with him? Brandy stared at Shaw, more unhappy than she had ever been in her life.

"I'll move out," she offered sadly.

"No need." He turned back to his closet, selecting shirts and slacks, pulling them off the hangers. "There are plenty of friends I can move in with to spare the hassle over the couch."

"But this is your home!"

"It hasn't felt like it since you moved in."

Brandy sniffed back the tears coming to her eyes. She had made such a mess of everything, all for the sake of a child. When they could be most happy that custody of Eric was not far away, they were most miserable with each other.

"I've always told you tears won't work on me."

"They're not for your benefit." She sniffed, wishing she had never set eyes on Shaw Janus.

"Good." He picked up his clothes. "And keep your feelings of love to yourself, stored away with those other conventions about marriage. They're outdated ideas anyway and have no stock with me. I don't believe in love, and I won't be influenced by that so-called emotion."

"It's your loss," Brandy wept, "and believe me, if I could deny my feelings as coldly as you can, I would. But I guess I'm just not as inhuman as you are, Shaw Janus. I'm warm and living and breathing because I feel. You're no warmer than a scaly old fish."

"You're entitled to your opinion." He threw his clothes over his arm. "I'll dress in the bathroom, if you don't mind."

"You don't have to, Shaw." Brandy stood up, buttoning her dress. "I'll sleep on the couch. You can have the bedroom again. It is, afterall, yours."

He turned and stared at her. "That's right. I'd almost forgotten."

Brandy collected the clothes she thought she would need in the morning and removed them from Shaw's closets, drawers and dresser while he showered.

She picked up the extra pillows from the closet to stuff between the cracks of the sofa in an effort to make it more comfortable. She was lucky he wasn't ready to throw her and Eric bodily out of the apartment. That he had agreed to continue with their charade of a marriage totally astounded her.

As she tossed and turned on the couch, trying to find a comfortable position, she realized what a mistake she had made with Shaw's life, her life, and Eric's life. What good would it do to gain custody of Eric, then uproot him from the kind of affection Shaw showed him? Wasn't that as emotionally damaging as if she had let Louis and May move him about the country? At least with them he would know the security of the same people.

The best thing she could do was to end this sham of a marriage, she realized. She had to leave Shaw. Before she could do that, she had to earn some money, and before that, get a new composite made. It all came back to money.

Then she thought of Marcus. He would help her. She remembered the kindly looks he had given her at the party, and the way he said he would be watching out for her. If she explained the situation to him, he would lend her the money for a good photographer. She would leave Shaw then, and give up this wild scheme of trying to get custody of Eric. As much as she wanted to keep him, she realized she could not do it alone. Whether Shaw was sitting legally beside her or not, she would be raising Eric alone, and it just would not work. A child needed a full time mother and father.

Brandy turned over, trying to find a dry place on the pillow to rest her head.

She couldn't blame Shaw. He had been good to them both and no one could have been kinder with Eric—taking him up in the airplane, playing games with him during his spare time from work, reading bedtime stories to him, and taking him to school. He was the perfect father. She had seen that in his personality, even if he could not. He was too stubborn to play the role of husband, and she couldn't do anything more to convince him that he would be wonderful in the part.

Nevertheless, as long as she still remained in this apartment, she would do everything she could to make life easy for him. She owed him that much, simply out of respect and gratitude.

But she wouldn't take advantage of his generosity any longer. She would speak to Marcus in the morning and start making plans to leave Shaw and live a life of independence.

Brandy woke early the next morning, grateful to straighten her back after a night curled on the couch. She busied herself in the kitchen, making little noise, and greeted Shaw as cheerfully as if they had spent the night together as the ideal couple.

She pretended to ignore his glaring glances, determined to make life as easy as possible for him. She had already interfered enough.

When they were ready to leave the apartment, Brandy offered to drive Eric to school herself, but Shaw wouldn't hear of it. His bright and cheerful attitude for Eric's benefit gave Brandy a slight ray of hope that maybe things could be worked out between them—but one penetratingly suspect glance from Shaw told her not to build pipe dreams.

It was over. She had to face it.

As soon as they left she began calling around town to locate Marcus, but he was nowhere to be found. She ended up leaving messages for him to return her call.

A week had passed before Brandy heard from Marcus. He had been out of town, he explained. In the meantime, Brandy's agent had managed to get her two short modeling assignments, providing her with some money of her own to use toward getting a photographer.

It was fortunate, she decided, that she was beginning to earn a little money again, since Marcus was not as helpful as she had expected him to be.

"Shaw will be livid when he hears what you're up to," Marcus warned.

"I don't understand why." Brandy defended her actions. "It's my life."

"Yes, but he never has exactly approved of your modeling."

"He hasn't told me that," Brandy huffed.

"Have you sat down and talked about it with him?"

"Of course not," Brandy said. Everytime they had come near the subject Shaw had skirted the issue, his anger making it impossible for her to discuss it sensibly with him. "Besides, it shouldn't make any difference to him once I leave him."

"Now what are you talking about?" Marcus demanded, his voice so like Shaw's over the phone that Brandy could almost imagine it was he.

"I'm going to leave Shaw. That's what this is all about."

"But you can't leave him!"

"Why not? He doesn't want me."

Marcus laughed, and Brandy wished she could see his face. Was he being cynical or sarcastic? "You don't know him."

"Exactly, but I do know I'm making him miserable and I—I care too much about him to continue inserting myself in his life when he doesn't want me there, no matter how good my intentions have been."

"Brandy," his voice began hysterically, then calmed. "Brandy, let's talk this out. You can't just suddenly remove yourself from his life."

"Why not? I'll leave the way I came." She was grateful she had caught a cold from sleeping in a draft on the couch, at least it had served some purpose. Her thick voice helped disguise her tears.

"But where will you go? What will you do?"

"I haven't thought that far ahead. Right now I just need some money to see a photographer. Then, I can take the photos to a printer, and the composite to an agent, and—"

"I have half a mind to tell Shaw about this," he interrupted.

"No, Marcus. It wouldn't do any good, and besides, I'm doing it for his sake. You just have to trust me about that. I wouldn't do anything to hurt him any more. He can go back to Lorraine and all her money and—"

"Now you really *are* talking nonsense." He laughed and Brandy thought he was trying to convince himself more than her. "Why anyone looking at the two of you couldn't help but see all the love between you."

"It's all an act, I tell you. He doesn't care one bit about me. I'm a liability. That's why I want to stop making him feel obligated to me. The only way I can do that is by modeling. I *can* stand on my own two feet, you know."

"Can you?" He paused, and Brandy's heart pounded waiting to hear what else he had to say. "If you could you wouldn't have to ask for a loan from me. Not that I wouldn't give it to you if I thought the reason were a good enough one. I just know how mad Shaw would be if he found out I had any part of this. So, I'm sorry, Brandy, but the answer is no. I'll help you anyway I can if you need me. But knowing what Shaw would say, I can't encourage your modeling."

Brandy's heart sagged. She had been so sure Marcus would help her. Now what would she do? Without realizing it, she began to run the possibilities over in her mind. "Well, I guess I can call Rex Henson. Some of the girls have mentioned him as being real easy to get around without much money, but he keeps strange hours. I'd have to get a babysitter for Eric. And—oh, never mind. I'll think of something, Marcus. I guess I can't blame you. I know how Shaw's temper can be. Thanks, anyway."

"Brandy—" His urgent voice made her stop from hanging up the phone. "Don't do anything without talking to Shaw first? Please? You might find you're underestimating him."

Chapter Eleven

Brandy gave Marcus' words some thought for a few days. She was finally convinced by the way Shaw glared at her whenever he came home, as if he couldn't wait to get her out of his sight. She felt as if he was plotting to get rid of her. He spent even less time at the apartment now, claiming work had him more bogged down than ever.

She called Rex Henson, the photographer some of the other girls had mentioned using, and arranged for a photo session. He kept odd hours, he said, and the only free time he had that week was at ten o'clock that night.

Brandy felt strange about traveling around the city on her own at that hour, but she needed the new composite, and Henson's price was within her means. She would have to get a sitter. She couldn't possibly ask Shaw to come home from his taxing business to watch Eric for one evening, not without explaining where she was going.

The more she thought about it, the more she realized how convenient the late night time would be, since Shaw, if he came home for dinner, would probably be gone again by eight o'clock and would never miss her.

Shaw seemed to eye her closer than ever that evening. She even caught him questioning Eric about what she had been doing lately, and what she was planning to do that night. Brandy was relieved that she had not told Eric the babysitter was coming. He should be fast asleep by that time, anyway.

After Shaw left, Brandy took her time packing a small suitcase with a variety of outfits to wear for her photos, and was ready to leave by the time the babysitter arrived.

It wasn't the usual girl, but the girl's grandmother. Brandy smiled at the dear little lady, thinking what a wonderful family her babysitter had: it wasn't the first time the girl had sent someone to pinch hit for her. Once it had been her mother, and another time her father. Brandy wished she and Shaw could make that kind of loving and caring family with Eric, but it was an impossible dream.

The photographer's studio was in the heart of the city, on one of the side streets off Peachtree Plaza. When Brandy drove past the address and saw the tiny entrance from an alley between two major buildings, she wished she had thought to bring someone with her. She was pushing the clock now at ten o'clock and he might be one of those temperamental photographers who thought his time was so precious he could not waste a minute of it.

She parked the car as close to the entrance as she could, retrieved her suitcase from the back seat, and tried the door. It was locked, but she noticed a tiny doorbell nearby and pushed it. The walls were too thick for her to hear the sound of the bell, so Brandy waited, then rang it again.

She was just about to knock on the heavy metal door when she heard someone undoing the bolts, and the door opened.

"Hello," her smile wavered on her face, "I'm Brandy."

He sized her up head to toe, shrugged, and said, "Come on in. Sorry about the door. I usually keep it unlatched when I'm expecting someone."

More than ever Brandy wished someone had come with her, but tried not to look nervous as he gestured for her to precede him through a warehouse-looking room dimly lit and stocked with everything from display posters to styrofoam mannequin heads—hundreds of them.

"What an interesting place," she gulped.

"It used to be a department store," he muttered and pointed her down a more brightly lit corridor to an open door on the left.

The room was large and filled with a photographer's studio equipment, backdrops, light stands, cameras on tripods, and shelves for accessories and film. She sighed and steadied her nerves a little. What could she expect for such a low price? she thought.

"You can change in there," he said curtly, and Brandy turned around, trying to see where he meant.

"The bathroom," he clarified when she didn't see any custom-made changing area.

"Okay," said Brandy, wishing now she had an ordinary job like a waitress or a nurse. She didn't like having to put her clothes on and off in cramped surroundings with a seedy little man standing just outside the door. She only hoped the lock worked.

It didn't.

Brandy propped her suitcase up against the door, so if he tried to make a pass at her, he might be stalled at least a few seconds by tripping over her suitcase before he could get to her. She shivered, picturing his hands as greasy as his swarthy complexion. She was letting her imagination run away with her, she told herself. It was the result of the past weeks of Shaw's overprotectiveness. Nothing had ever happened to her before, she thought, and there was no reason to think anything would now. Besides, she was too short.

She emerged wearing a pair of designer jeans and a western blouse in colors flattering to her complexion.

The photographer turned from loading one of his cameras with film, looked at Brandy, and asked, "When are you going to change?"

"I just did."

He shrugged again. "Could have fooled me. You look almost the same as when you came in. That outfit is as tacky as a sack. Don't you have something that will show off your—personality a little better?"

"I'll see," said Brandy, suddenly nervous again. They weren't getting off to a very smooth start. Maybe he was just difficult with everyone he photographed.

She took longer this time and picked out a dress with wide skirts and a narrow waist, making her resemble a Southern belle. It had a gathered neckline that could be worn slightly off the shoulder. She wasn't surprised at all when Henson asked her to slip the material off her shoulders a bit for a more revealing neckline. Brandy did as she was told out of habit. He was, after all, a professional photographer: it was his job to make her look good for the camera. She didn't want to look, as he had implied, like a nine-year-old.

He took a long time with the photos, teaching her different poses: skirt in her hands, bending over with her hands on her knees, and over the shoulder glances. As roll after roll of film clicked through his expensive cameras, Brandy began to feel she was getting more than her money's worth; he had quoted her a fixed fee for the time and rolls of film he spent on her.

"Let's take a break." He came to the end of another roll of film and stretched. "Thirsty?"

"A little," she admitted. Studio lights were always blazing hot, except in the dead of winter when swimsuits were modeled.

"Why don't you go change into something else while I fix something? Orange juice okay?"

"Fine." She smiled, beginning to feel if not rapport with the man, at least less uneasy.

"Let's see something this time that shows off your legs. I have an idea that's going to be one of your assets."

Brandy wasn't about to argue with him. Everyone had told her she had lovely legs, but because she was so short, she was never called for the leggy style of fashion shot.

She changed into a sporty outfit of coordinated terry and hoped the photographer would find it satisfactory.

He didn't comment as he handed her a chilled glass of orange juice. He waited until she had finished her drink, looking at his watch frequently enough to make her feel again that she was taking up too much of his time. He shot several more rolls of film of Brandy in various poses, until she felt herself falling into a routine: front foot forward—hand on hip—quarter turn—throw head back—half turn—down on one knee —tilt head to the right—stand again—run tongue around lips—quarter turn—glance over shoulder. It was all rather dizzying, but fun. She was feeling looser with him, and he seemed to feel so, too, because he began mumbling, "Good, good . . . beautiful . . . that's it . . . a little more to the left . . . perfect." The film raced through the camera.

"Now—" He smiled, as he finished another roll of film. "Let's try something seductive. You have a sexy look that we could develop. It'll show that you have a variety of looks, which could be quite a selling point for your composite."

Brandy hesitated. "Well, all right." He was the professional, she thought. He had probably done hundreds of composites for models. He should know what he was talking about.

When she emerged wearing a wraparound gown that she thought was rather attractive, he frowned. "Terrible! Worse than a Hawaiian muu-muu! Don't you have anything more revealing?"

"Just a swimsuit," Brandy said.

He shook his head, indicating she had fallen out of his graces after his delight with the last few frames. "It'll have to do, I guess. Hey," he smiled, when he saw how disappointed she looked that she had not brought the kind of clothes he wanted, "how about another drink? I've been working you pretty hard."

Brandy smiled at his gesture of friendship. "Thanks. I'd like that."

Her swimsuit, for all that it revealed, was fairly demure. It was the one she wore in public whenever she had an invitation to go swimming; she had another for tanning. They went through the routine again, the photographer feeling more pleased with each whirr of his fast moving shutter. Brandy was becoming more confident in front of him, giggling at his jokes, until he straightened and said, "Let's try a bareback shot."

"A what?"

"Take your top off. Let's see what you look like. Glance over your shoulder at me. It should be very seductive."

Also very embarrassing, she thought.

"I don't know. Is this necessary? I don't think I'd like that kind of photo on my composite."

He sighed. "You're probably a little nervous, right?"

She nodded, glad that he understood.

He smiled a friendly smile. "If it makes you feel any better, most girls feel that way. But believe me, they all end up doing it sooner or later. The sooner they do it, the better their career becomes."

Brandy bit her lip. He was a professional. He dealt with models all day and all night. "I just don't know," she said hesitantly.

"Look—" His grin widened. "There's nobody here but you and me. Just turn your back on me and unsnap your top. I won't even see anything!" He paused. "Let's just try one. If you don't like it, we won't use it in the final composite."

That seemed reasonable enough. And what could he do to her from all the way across the room? She turned her back to him, hesitating, suddenly wondering why she felt so sleepy and dizzy. It was late. The sooner she did what he asked, the sooner they would be finished and she could go home.

"Come on now." He laughed to put her at ease. "Don't be shy. Just unsnap the thing and let it drop."

"Don't you dare!" An all too familiar voice shattered Brandy's haze and startled the photographer. She spun around to see Shaw standing in the doorway.

"Who the hell are you?" demanded the photographer, all pretense of friendliness disappearing as his brows furrowed at the interruption. "How did you get in here?"

"Walked in," said Shaw. "Brandy, get dressed."

"See here," bristled the photographer, "what right do you have to come in here disrupting a professional session?"

"It doesn't look like anything professional to me!" thundered Shaw. "Brandy, do as I say."

"Listen, buddy, this happens to be my studio, and as I see it, you're trespassing!"

Shaw took several steps into the studio. His angry glance at Brandy made her scurry for the protection of her clothes and the bathroom. She could hear his powerful voice even with the door slammed shut behind her. "One minute later and it would have been you who would have been trespassing, buster," he practically shouted. "That's my wife, and I have no doubt as to your intentions, even if she did."

"Your wife?"

"That's right—as in married—as in you'll be sorry if she so much as tells me you touched her. Did you?"

Brandy imagined Shaw hauling the little man up by

the throat of his shirt, as she heard his next reply garbled. She struggled into her jeans and shirt, and stuffed her other clothes into her suitcase.

Whatever Shaw was doing, she knew he meant business, and she wondered half fearfully what sort of punishment would be in store for her when she got home. She knew he would treat her more like a small child than like his wife. She wasn't looking forward to the next moments alone with him. It was bad enough that he had found her here and was harassing that poor photographer. She would probably never get her composite done at this rate.

"Brandy!" He pounded on the door. "Aren't you ready yet?"

"Yes," she half whispered, and she opened the door, clutching her suitcase, which was jammed closed with a shirt-sleeve hanging out.

His hand grasped Brandy's like a vise as he hauled her across the room. She tried to apologize to the photographer for Shaw's behavior, but she was so shocked by the whirlwind of circumstances that all she could do was follow Shaw open-mouthed as he hauled her out the door.

He pushed Brandy into her car and tossed the suitcase into the back. "Now stay in this car until you get to the apartment—and don't try anything funny because I'll be driving right behind you. We're going to have this out once and for all."

Brandy nodded, still unable to utter a word in the face of his anger.

She was apprehensive during the drive home and amazed that she wasn't colliding with anything—her mind was on everything but driving.

He was tight-lipped and forceful as he hauled her

through the lobby and into the elevator, as if she would dare try to go anywhere else, whether he was holding her or not.

He unlocked the apartment door and put on his kindest face for the babysitter, payed her generously for her time, and ushered her to her apartment in the building, his eyes warning Brandy before he left that she had better be on the sofa when he returned.

She had nowhere to go. If she were going to leave Shaw, she had to do it openly. No one would get away with fooling Shaw Janus about anything. She hadn't with this marriage. When he came back, she would tell him she wanted an annulment and she would not ask for any support or alimony from him. She would just have to give Eric to Louis and May. They, at least, could provide some semblance of a home for him.

When Shaw came back he continued to glare at her, and took his time pouring a drink before he came to stand in front of her. "Well?"

"Well what?" she snapped back, feeling very tired, very alone, very sad.

"What do you have to say for yourself?" he challenged.

She glared up at him, all the way to his taunting eyes. "I'm ready for that annulment."

He raised his brows, and she imagined that his color paled slightly. "Then you've changed your mind?" he asked.

"About what?"

"About what you told me the other night . . . about what you've told me all along about wanting to make a home for Eric . . . about needing a husband . . . about loving me."

Tears pricked behind her eyes, and she shook her head. "No. I meant every bit of that."

"Then why the annulment?" He finished off his drink and poured another.

"Because I'm destroying you. You don't want me. You never did."

"Don't tell me what I want or don't want!" he flared. "I never said I didn't want you, lady."

Brandy sniffed. "Yes, that was obvious, but what I meant was love. Love is important to me, but it means nothing to you. And it can't really be love if it's hurting those involved."

He sat down on the sectional sofa adjacent, but not near, to her. "That's true. I never wanted love. I didn't believe in it. I'd never known what it was."

She shrugged, tears dripping down her cheeks. "I know. I realize I can't expect you to magically feel the way I do. You either care or you don't."

He slid a little closer—close enough to take her chin in his hand and turn her face to him. "I care." His voice was husky. "I care a lot."

She shook her head, unable to believe him.

He forced her chin to stay still, and waited until she was looking at him. "But it's new to me," he continued, "I'm just beginning to feel alive. And I know it would kill me if you left us, Brandy."

"Us?"

"Eric and me. Marcus told me what you had in mind."

"Oh!"

"Don't get mad at him. He made me realize what you mean to me. Just the thought of you leaving has been tearing me up these last few days, but I've been so busy I kept telling myself I could put off talking to you.

But when I came in tonight and found that strange woman here, and she said you'd packed a suitcase, I nearly went crazy. Marcus didn't know where you'd gone, but he remembered you mentioning that guy's name and I took a chance you'd be with him."

"You don't want me to go?" Her eyes were shimmering with tears.

"Oh, baby." He pulled her into his arms. "I need you. I want you. I think I must love you. I only know I've never known I could feel as violent as I did this evening when I realized how close I'd come to losing you. And that photographer—" She could feel his body trembling. "When I think that he almost stole your sweet innocence, and when it's been here for me, offered as a gift of love all this time. I was too cynical to think I could survive with one woman."

"I can understand if you can't."

He laughed. "That's a switch, coming after your accusations that I've been spending my nights with Lorraine. I haven't, you know."

"But she said—"

"Don't believe a word of what she says. She's spoiled and it won't be the first time she's lied to get her way."

"But she said she would break you financially if I didn't leave you to her!"

He laughed at that, too. "So what? Would you mind very much if we had to live in a more modest place? If it takes me a little longer to make it to the top?"

She shook her head, still wondering if she were dreaming it all. She was still feeling dizzy and sleepy. Orange juice alone had never made her feel this way.

"Good," he said, "because whatever happens, wherever we live, whatever we do, it'll be together. I know now how miserable it would be to live without you after these past weeks of living with you." He sighed. "I can't begin to tell you the number of nights I wished I could stay here with you instead of going back to that blasted restaurant."

"But you love it."

"I love you more." He squeezed her. "But I'm afraid the restaurant is still going to be taking up a lot of my time until I can get it operating. Can you take me that way for awhile?"

"What way?"

"On a part-time basis."

"Oh, Shaw." She hugged him, her sobs in earnest now. "I'll take you anyway I can get you. I love you, I told you that."

"I know," he smiled, "and it's been preying on my mind ever since. Do you know how much a coward that made me feel?"

"I don't understand."

"To know that you had the courage to tell me how you felt about me. But I was too busy trying to be the big macho male to think my emotions could get the better of me. Oh, baby, don't cry. You know I can't stand it when you do. It makes me feel so helpless."

She hugged him. "I can't stop crying. All I want is to be with you."

"You will be, my love, for all time. Now stop crying before *I* start."

Brandy laughed through her tears and then caught her breath to discover that he was actually crying, too! Somehow that made him seem her equal, not an arrogant lord who would always get the better of her, but someone just as vulnerable as she. It only made her love him more.

She put her hands up to his cheeks, cradling his face between her hands. He had just admitted he was as human and just as frightened of her love as she. She had never realized how much power, the power of love, she held in her hands.

Gently she kissed him, the tenderness between them quickly mounting to passion. Brandy sighed against his lips. This was the moment she had waited for. She belonged to Shaw, and had from the first moment she had seen him and decided she wanted him for a husband. She had sensed even then the melting heat of his kisses, but nothing had prepared her for the weakness of her body as it pressed closer to his, meeting his passion with a sultry sexiness that she had not known herself capable of.

His lips trailed down her cheek to her neck as he murmured against her skin, "I want to make love to you, wife."

His words sent little flames of excitement through her.

"Will you share my bed with me?"

In answer Brandy stood up, tugging him after her to the bedroom. He could be so tender and caring. She had known it in her heart long before tonight. Perhaps he hadn't even realized his own tenderness and consideration before this moment. He was not demanding she share his bed as he had done in the past. He was humbling himself by asking her.

"Show me, Shaw." She wrapped her arms around his neck as they reached the bedroom. "Teach me how to love you."

He chuckled against her ear where his lips were nibbling on her earlobe. "You already know how to do that, my love. In fact, I think I should be taking lessons from you."

She wound her fingers into his hair, unable to get close enough to him. "Well, we could begin tonight—"

He kicked the door shut. "Exactly what I had in mind," he whispered.

IT'S YOUR OWN SPECIAL TIME

Contemporary romances for today's women.
Each month, six very special love stories will be yours
from SILHOUETTE. Look for them wherever books are sold
or order now from the coupon below.

$1.50 each

☐ 5 Goforth	☐ 28 Hampson	☐ 54 Beckman	☐ 83 Halston
☐ 6 Stanford	☐ 29 Wildman	☐ 55 LaDame	☐ 84 Vitek
☐ 7 Lewis	☐ 30 Dixon	☐ 56 Trent	☐ 85 John
☐ 8 Beckman	☐ 32 Michaels	☐ 57 John	☐ 86 Adams
☐ 9 Wilson	☐ 33 Vitek	☐ 58 Stanford	☐ 87 Michaels
☐ 10 Caine	☐ 34 John	☐ 59 Vernon	☐ 88 Stanford
☐ 11 Vernon	☐ 35 Stanford	☐ 60 Hill	☐ 89 James
☐ 17 John	☐ 38 Browning	☐ 61 Michaels	☐ 90 Major
☐ 19 Thornton	☐ 39 Sinclair	☐ 62 Halston	☐ 92 McKay
☐ 20 Fulford	☐ 46 Stanford	☐ 63 Brent	☐ 93 Browning
☐ 22 Stephens	☐ 47 Vitek	☐ 71 Ripy	☐ 94 Hampson
☐ 23 Edwards	☐ 48 Wildman	☐ 73 Browning	☐ 95 Wisdom
☐ 24 Healy	☐ 49 Wisdom	☐ 76 Hardy	☐ 96 Beckman
☐ 25 Stanford	☐ 50 Scott	☐ 78 Oliver	☐ 97 Clay
☐ 26 Hastings	☐ 52 Hampson	☐ 81 Roberts	☐ 98 St. George
☐ 27 Hampson	☐ 53 Browning	☐ 82 Dailey	☐ 99 Camp

$1.75 each

☐ 100 Stanford	☐ 110 Trent	☐ 120 Carroll	☐ 130 Hardy
☐ 101 Hardy	☐ 111 South	☐ 121 Langan	☐ 131 Stanford
☐ 102 Hastings	☐ 112 Stanford	☐ 122 Scofield	☐ 132 Wisdom
☐ 103 Cork	☐ 113 Browning	☐ 123 Sinclair	☐ 133 Rowe
☐ 104 Vitek	☐ 114 Michaels	☐ 124 Beckman	☐ 134 Charles
☐ 105 Eden	☐ 115 John	☐ 125 Bright	☐ 135 Logan
☐ 106 Dailey	☐ 116 Lindley	☐ 126 St. George	☐ 136 Hampson
☐ 107 Bright	☐ 117 Scott	☐ 127 Roberts	☐ 137 Hunter
☐ 108 Hampson	☐ 118 Dailey	☐ 128 Hampson	☐ 138 Wilson
☐ 109 Vernon	☐ 119 Hampson	☐ 129 Converse	☐ 139 Vitek

$1.75 each

☐ 140 Erskine	☐ 161 Trent	☐ 181 Terrill	☐ 201 Starr
☐ 142 Browning	☐ 162 Ashby	☐ 182 Clay	☐ 202 Hampson
☐ 143 Roberts	☐ 163 Roberts	☐ 183 Stanley	☐ 203 Browning
☐ 144 Goforth	☐ 164 Browning	☐ 184 Hardy	☐ 204 Carroll
☐ 145 Hope	☐ 165 Young	☐ 185 Hampson	☐ 205 Maxam
☐ 146 Michaels	☐ 166 Wisdom	☐ 186 Howard	☐ 206 Manning
☐ 147 Hampson	☐ 167 Hunter	☐ 187 Scott	☐ 207 Windham
☐ 148 Cork	☐ 168 Carr	☐ 188 Cork	☐ 208 Halston
☐ 149 Saunders	☐ 169 Scott	☐ 189 Stephens	☐ 209 LaDame
☐ 150 Major	☐ 170 Ripy	☐ 190 Hampson	☐ 210 Eden
☐ 151 Hampson	☐ 171 Hill	☐ 191 Browning	☐ 211 Walters
☐ 152 Halston	☐ 172 Browning	☐ 192 John	☐ 212 Young
☐ 153 Dailey	☐ 173 Camp	☐ 193 Trent	☐ 213 Dailey
☐ 154 Beckman	☐ 174 Sinclair	☐ 194 Barry	☐ 214 Hampson
☐ 155 Hampson	☐ 175 Jarrett	☐ 195 Dailey	☐ 215 Roberts
☐ 156 Sawyer	☐ 176 Vitek	☐ 196 Hampson	☐ 216 Saunders
☐ 157 Vitek	☐ 177 Dailey	☐ 197 Summers	☐ 217 Vitek
☐ 158 Reynolds	☐ 178 Hampson	☐ 198 Hunter	☐ 218 Hunter
☐ 159 Tracy	☐ 179 Beckman	☐ 199 Roberts	☐ 219 Cork
☐ 160 Hampson	☐ 180 Roberts	☐ 200 Lloyd	

$1.95 each

___#220 THE DAWN IS GOLDEN, Hampson   ___#226 SWEET SECOND LOVE, Hampson
___#221 PRACTICAL DREAMER, Browning   ___#227 FORBIDDEN AFFAIR, Beckman
___#222 TWO FACES OF LOVE, Carroll   ___#228 DANCE AT YOUR WEDDING, King
___#223 A PRIVATE EDEN, Summers   ___#229 FOR ERIC'S SAKE, Thornton
___#224 HIDDEN ISLE, Langan   ___#230 IVORY INNOCENCE, Stevens
___#225 DELTA RIVER MAGIC, St. George   ___#231 WESTERN MAN, Dailey

Silhouette Romance

15-Day Free Trial Offer
6 Silhouette Romances

6 Silhouette Romances, free for 15 days! We'll send you 6 new Silhouette Romances to keep for 15 days, absolutely free! If you decide not to keep them, send them back to us. You pay nothing.

Free Home Delivery. But if you enjoy them as much as we think you will, keep them by paying the invoice enclosed with your free trial shipment. We'll pay all shipping and handling charges. You get the convenience of Home Delivery and we pay the postage and handling charge each month.

Don't miss a copy. The Silhouette Book Club is the way to make sure you'll be able to receive every new romance we publish before they're sold out. There is no minimum number of books to buy and you can cancel at any time.

This offer expires December 31, 1983